I0835259

DIRT

A NOVEL BY

ERICA FRIEDLAND TUFARO

Ten|16
PRESS

Dirt

SC ISBN: 9781645386421

eBook ISBN: 9781645386438

Dirt
By Erica Friedland Tufaro

Cover design by Dana Breunig

Line separator by Alenast/stock.adobe.com

Published by Ten16 Press, an imprint of Orange Hat Publishing

Ten16 Press
Wauwatosa, WI

For more information, visit orangehatpublishing.com

DEDICATION

For those who dare to swim against the tide, remember to keep your head up and never stop kicking!

AUTHOR'S NOTE

This story is fiction inspired by real events. I was on a dig at Aphrodisias in 1998, and experienced many of the emotions felt by the main character Ally Acker at the time. However, I took a great deal of liberty with the characters and the plot. I have been wanting to write this story since my return. I had to wait until COVID to find the time and motivation to tell it. It has been my pleasure to go back in time before COVID, before kids, before smartphones, before even 9/11. Reflecting back on myself then, I laughed and cried to recall who I was. It was touching to remember my innocence and naivety, as well as my fearlessness, and realize how life and time have changed me. I was surprised to discover I could recapture some of my youthful courage and draw on it to face the present and future. Enjoy.

CHAPTER 1

FLIGHT

A muffled voice over the PA system indicated the flight to Istanbul was delayed two hours. Two more hours with Phyllis and Howard in the JFK terminal. Two more cigarette-free hours listening to their reservations regarding my decision to travel to Turkey alone. I was headed to the ancient city of Aphrodisias, dedicated to the goddess of love. I had won a fellowship to join art historians and archeologists there. I would be working as an architect documenting monuments on the famous site. My ticket plus room and board would be covered, plus a small stipend. I was an adult, and my parents couldn't say no. I wasn't asking them for anything this time except a ride to the airport, and right now I was regretting even that.

Upon arrival in Istanbul, I was connecting to the city of Izmir and then continuing by bus to the dig site near the ancient western town of Geyre. Someone called Henry from the dig was to meet me at the airport in Izmir and travel with me to the site. How he would find me, I was still not certain. This was 1998. Who had a cell phone? And if you did, who had international service? And even if you did, there was no cell service where I was headed. Phyllis and Howard were starting to freak me out.

I felt very self-conscious as a Shebrew without a chaperone in a Muslim country, and my parents had said or done nothing to bolster my self-confidence. Five more minutes of them catastrophizing, and there was no way I was getting on that plane. And I needed to get on that plane. I needed to get away. All year the pressure had been building, and I was getting crushed beneath it.

My sister had just given birth a week after my graduation to the first grandchild. Meanwhile, I was twenty-six, unemployed, and without prospects, both personal and professional. And I had to forgo travel at the tail end of my seven-week commitment to the dig to make an appearance at two different sorority sisters' weddings at the end of August.

The ink on my master of architecture was not yet dry, and already I felt an overwhelming sense of failure. Despite my glorious and potentially lucrative pedigree as a business major at Penn who graduated with honors, I had lost my way and was pursuing an alternative lifestyle as an "artist." I needed to find like-minded lost souls with whom to commune. I needed validation. Some time away would give me clarity and perspective. A summer spent amongst these academics from all over the globe would be inspirational, transformative, and, not least of all put a respectable pause on my job search.

I wasn't running away, arms wide open into the unknown. I was more slinking off and looking for cover. This all seemed a romantic notion eight months ago when the onslaught of engagements and a pregnancy announcement, in addition to my thesis, were making me fidgety. I had taken up briefly with Philip from my class before Christmas simply to blow off steam while locking onto my thesis project. We were really just friends and should have just stayed friends. But restlessness is a dangerous aphrodisiac. So there you go. He had done the Turkey trip the summer before and was planning another summer at the dig. It was tempting, and the thought of having some romantic company on this exotic adventure was even more enticing. I was always a great lover of mythology and the classics. I was the twelve-year-old kid reading the *Meridian Book of Myths* or the *Odyssey* on the beach in Mexico. This would be perfect. Right on brand. Based on everything that had ever happened to me, I should have known better.

Now the romance with Philip was ancient history, and I was beginning to question the wisdom of this entire plan. The usual dark cloud of self-doubt was overhead. I wasn't sure I could do this. Not any part of it. No. I wouldn't go. I would tell Phyllis and Howard I just couldn't leave the family right now. I shouldn't be traveling alone, a woman, a Jewish woman, to a Muslim country. My parents would be thrilled. They would call the dig and get me out of it...say I was ill or something. Howard would make a donation. I eyed my mother. She was nervously twisting a lock of her shoulder-length dark hair and discreetly nibbling at her inside cheek. Our eyes locked. She was thinking the same thing.

Suddenly, a voice called my flight, and I was running toward security. P and H were waving frantically enough to dishevel their coordinating summer-weight cashmere pastel cardigans. The duty-free bag with the two cartons of Dunhills I had secretly bought on a bathroom run was being crushed inside my daypack as it bounced up and down against the back of my head, nearly knocking off the umbrella-sized Audrey Hepburn–style sun hat that I would have to hold the whole eleven-hour flight to keep it from being smushed. The anti-anxiety pill I had popped twenty minutes ago to help me get on the plane was kicking in, and my body felt like it weighed two thousand pounds.

Flustered, I threw the documents at the flight attendant and stepped onto the gangway, turning back for one last look at my parents before boarding. They stood frozen, their eyes wide with terror, their hands clapped over their mouths. I made my way to coach as the last call announcement hung in the air. Strapping myself in, I stared out the window, hoping whoever was assigned to sit next to me would not attempt to interact. Hardly visible beneath my spectacular hat, I pretended to be asleep when a body plopped into the adjacent seat. The plane began to move and was in the air within minutes. Everything was behind me now.

I woke with a start two hours later. I was being watched. Six eyes blinked too close to my face. Two belonged to the guy next to me, and another pair to a man leaning over him. The last two were on the face of an exotic-looking flight attendant with what looked like a fez bobby pinned to her tight bun. They were all trying to shake a dinner order out of me. I could not understand the options, so I asked for a roll and a glass of wine. I had no idea what they ate in Turkey, and while I was pretty sure pork was not on the menu, I had no other clues, and of course, I was trying to avoid a fattening choice. There was a good bit of back and forth and confusion. I had to explain my order to an additional airline employee and two passengers, clearly just wanting to be part of the action. Finally, another fez-topped attendant set a tray in front of me with two small bottles of wine, two fresh rolls, and a plate of something oozing syrup from every pore. "Baklava!" she exclaimed proudly with a smile. Well, I knew what that was, and it was certainly not on Weight Watchers, but when in Rome, so to speak. Anyway, it was clear they'd brought the bread and dessert from first class. It was considerate, and I did not want to be rude.

After two bottles of wine and the sugary plate, my head was spinning. A question came my way from my smiling neighbor. I did not understand, so I dumbly smiled back. He tried again, pointing at my sticky, empty plate and rubbing his doughy belly, making yummy noises. I laughed and nodded.

"Yes, yes. I love Baklava."

He said something else and pointed to himself. He repeated "Hakan, Hakan!" and again gestured toward his chest and then pointed to me.

"Ah, Hakan." I parroted, pointing to him and then said, "Ally," tapping my own chest. This seemed to impress him.

"Ah, Ali, you Turk?" He pronounced my name Ali as in Muhammad Ali.

"No, American."

"You Turk. Okay, Ali. Sigara?"

I blinked, and he signed like he was smoking. Thank God. "Yes, yes. Thank you! Sigara, yes." I reached for the Dunhills and followed him to the back of the plane.

The smoking section on my flight was like fucking Ibiza. The smoke cloud was thick, music playing, and I could have sworn somewhere there was a cobra winding out of a basket. The partygoers seemed happy to see us. Hakan found some people he knew and introduced me.

"Altan, Efe, Banu," and then back to me, "Ali." Everyone nodded at me, and Altan got up to give me his seat. Banu was about my age and spoke English. I was surprised to see she did not cover her head. Her medium brown hair fell halfway down her back and moved a lot when she spoke. Her hazel eyes matched those of Efe, who I learned was her brother. The other two were friends of his from home. They met Hakan in school in the US. They all had been studying at NYU last term. They were going to party first in Bodrum before heading home for the summer.

We all chain-smoked and nibbled on pistachios from Banu's purse, spitting the seeds on her tray table. Finally, Efe cracked open a bottle of something from the duty-free that smelled like licorice and started to pour out shots for me and the gang. A few other passengers caught a whiff and sent around empty cups. We all clanged cups, and the Turks knocked back the whole shot cheering "Serefe!" I gingerly took a small sip. The liquor burned my throat.

"Raki!" Banu boomed and refilled their cups. I smiled and shook my head as they emptied their glasses and toasted again. They asked me a hundred questions regarding my ethnicity as well as my reason for traveling, Banu translating. They all knew of the site as well as others on the west coast, some more famous, some less. They seemed unphased that they were all Greek ruins, technically from the time when the Roman Empire ruled the Greek world. I always thought the Turks and Greeks were enemies. I expected them to spit on the floor when I told them where I was going. Instead, they were very proud. On the other hand, they had plenty to say about the English, digging up their national treasures and dragging them back to London Museums. Interesting. They had more in common with the Greeks than they knew.

Efe asked Banu something and nodded towards me. "Ali," asked Efe, "are you sure you're not a Turk? You look Turk." He gestured at my almost black hair and tanned skin.

"Uhh, no."

"Italian? Spanish?" Banu continued to probe. She

exchanged words with Efe.

"Greek? Kurd?" Aside from the Greeks, I also remembered something about the Turks having beef with the Kurds. I decided that might be worse than the truth.

"No. I'm—I am Jewish. Hebrew." I wasn't sure which translated better. "Yahudi!" said Banu, and they all nodded.

"Yahudi is a good people. Turk peoples always like," said Efe.

"During the Inquisition, five hundred thousand came from Spain and were welcomed. And again, in World War II, Turkey protected the Jews," Banu explained. Hm. I did not know that. My mother had a laminated list of every nation, ethnicity, or individual who has ever either helped or harmed a Jew. It was on the "B" side of the list of my Bat Mitzvah attendees and the monetary gifts they gave. I need to make sure she had credited the Ottoman Empire for their fair deeds during the Middle Ages.

We chatted and signed back and forth. The gang gave me the highlights of Turkey, including Discotheque Halikarnas, apparently a legendary club in Bodrum. Not really my speed, but I nodded and smiled. They also insisted I visit Ayvalik, a Turkish seaside resort town on the Aegean coast consisting of a series of islands.

"It's like Turkish 'Amptoms, but the water is warm like piss," said Banu. Charming.

After another hour of sipping raki and chain smoking, my head ached. As a bonus, the sweet dessert and hard liquor were not sitting well in my stomach. I told my friends I was tired, yawning and rubbing my eyes to negate the need for translation and tip-toed in the dark back to my seat. So far, the prospect of Turkey seemed more promising than I had anticipated. A warm water Hamptons and booming nightlife? I could get behind that. I guzzled a two-liter Evian purchased in the airport and passed out.

I dreamt I was on the beach somewhere. It was an ocean beach, judging by the surf. I was at a wedding, except the Rabbi wasn't speaking Hebrew. It was Turkish, maybe? Anyway, I was wearing my stupid hat, and the wind blew me right into the water! But instead of freezing, it was warm like a bathtub. My whole family was on the shore yelling my name and waving me in, but I didn't swim toward them. Instead, I turned and swam toward the horizon. The sunlight was blazing, so I closed my eyes and blindly swam away.

CHAPTER 2

RUDE AWAKENING

This time when I opened my eyes, Hakan was back, and he was poking me and pointing out of the window. "Istanbul, Ali. Istanbul!" I was kind of hoping my posse would be traveling all the way to Izmir and would offer to escort me to Geyre, the village where the site was located. Alas, I was on my own. I excused myself and hit the restroom to brush my teeth and make myself presentable. While I was only twenty-six and could still knock them back with the best of them, I felt like shit and didn't look much better. The shaky landing didn't help. The pilot seemed to have the same technique for landing that I had for parallel parking back in The City: hit the rear, tap the front, and wiggle in.

Finally, we were on the ground, and the Turks seemed as excited to disembark as they were last night in the smoking section. My friends all hugged me and wished me luck, shouting "Gule, gule!" which I assumed was "Good-bye," and suddenly I was alone. I checked the spelling and number of my connection and headed for the gate. I needed coffee. A lot.

I found a kiosk near my gate with a sign that read "Kahve" and had a picture of a little cup. Eureka. "Kahve?" I asked the bare-headed barista whose face looked like an icon.

"Sade? Az şekerli? Orta şekerli? Çok şekerli?" she fired back. Devil.

I stared blankly back at her, and her smile disappeared. She asked again louder. "Sade? Az şekerli? Orta şekerli? Çok şekerli?" Oy. Was this a size question? I needed the biggest one, so I repeated the last thing she said.

"Çok şekerli, please."

She nodded, and her smile returned. "Lütfen," she said.

I parroted "Lütfen." A good bit of whizzing from the machine, and she handed me a thimble of dark liquid.

"Teşekkür ederim," she nodded again, and I repeated in tears at the size of my coffee. I shot it back in one sip. Did they list the sizes in reverse order here, or maybe there were even smaller portions? The taste kicked in instantly, and I winced. It was strong as hell, almost sweeter than the baklava. She took my reaction as pleasure and continued to nod and smile happily. I immediately hit an ATM for some Turkish lira. The thought of another exchange with a local resulting in perhaps the accidental purchase of a bottle of raki had me in search of a vending machine for some water. My head was pounding, and I didn't want to deal.

Before I knew it, my connection was called, and I was herded onto a much smaller plane. This group looked far more "local" than the passengers headed for Istanbul. I half expected a goat to take the seat across from me and could swear I heard a chicken clucking from a carry-on toward the rear of the plane. My headache subsided a bit, so I tried to sort out what I was doing on this trip. Clearly, I was avoiding the inevitability of full-time employment. That was obvious. Additionally, the reality that all of my college friends were moving on and up with their lives in The City had me feeling a little insecure. But what else?

I had always loved history, particularly ancient history, art history, and obviously architecture. Further, at school, I had always been a great success. With the exception of graduate school, I had always been the straight-A student, teacher's pet, top of the class. I always felt validated by this. I knew who I was and what I was worth. I guess I was looking to bask in the safety of academia for a little longer. This was a bold move. It would be a little basic, but I had been on two American Trails West teen tours back in the eighties. One of which was all camping. Plus, I had driven across the country with my college bestie, Mel, and lived out of my Honda Prelude for four weeks. I could rough it with the best of them. I would return refreshed, empowered, and able to face my future.

I thought about the thing with Philip. My graduate program was lonely and isolating, and more than once, I made a friend who turned out wanting more. It never ended well, and I never looked great on the other side. I just didn't want any entanglements. I didn't want anyone else's dreams clouding my vision. I was going back to New York to make my own way on my own terms. I neither wanted nor needed any background noise making me doubt. Apparently, guys don't like being shrugged off when no longer wanted any more than girls do. Noted.

Meanwhile, the thought of facing seven weeks of awkwardness with Philip was suddenly filling me with dread. Until then, I had pushed it aside, much like I had Philip. It was a little thing. Just a month or two. He didn't take it well. I hoped he wasn't holding a grudge. He was the only person I knew on this dig and had been my friend before. I shook it off again and closed my eyes as the plane rattled into the air.

I guess it was jet lag, or maybe the hangover, but I drifted off to sleep again. This time I dreamed I was standing on a wall in a full burqa. A crowd gathered behind me. As I sketched and worked, a tour guide explained, "This woman was rejected by her village. She refused a path that led to a good job, secure future, and marriage to a lawyer. Why? She has a romantic and stupid idea that she has choices in life. She now must cover herself entirely because her family is ashamed of her." The group seemed to be bending down to pick up stones that littered the ground.

A baby was screaming. Or maybe it was me? We touched down on the tarmac in Izmir. Before I knew it, I had navigated the airport lines and collected my backpack from the baggage claim. And there I was. Sweaty and hungover. And I was alone. I stood, head spinning in my Jackie O shades and my absurd hat squinting into the blinding sun. A voice was calling my name. Was it God? Was I dead?

A slight, balding man was headed my way and waving and calling. "Ally!"

There was not even a question in his voice. It was as if no other person on Earth arriving in Izmir has, could, or would look more like Ally Acker, of the Upper East Side of Manhattan, daughter of Phyllis and Howard Acker. I suddenly felt like Fran Drescher from *The Nanny*.

"Ally. Hi, I'm Henry Katz. From the dig."

Ahh. A fellow tribesman. It was a good omen. He smiled genuinely and shook my hand.

"Hi, Henry. How did you recognize me?"

"I have a copy of your passport."

Well, that explained it. I felt a little less conspicuous. I noticed how fair and freckled he was. Feeling the relentless sun already scorching down, I made a mental note to pray for him.

"Are you all set? Trip was okay? Sorry we have to hustle. The bus is leaving in a few minutes, and the next one isn't for hours."

He had his own pack, so he made no move to help me with mine. I looked around for a porter to wave over when he yanked my arm and started sprinting toward the bus depot near the airport entrance.

It had to be a hundred degrees by now, and I was schvitzing like mad! I huffed and puffed with the forty pounds of crap strapped to my back and front. So much for the Lotte Burke Method building core strength. Finally, we stopped, and Henry tore the pack from my back and shoved me into a minivan. I struggled to see behind me. I needed to see my luggage get onto the bus, as per Howard Acker's school of travel, and came face to face with a baby sheep or lamb. The lamb's person was a stooped woman with a covered head. She looked disapprovingly at my hat, which I had to cram between my legs to fit on the bus. Henry jumped on next to me, wiping his face with a bandana. And we were off!

Everyone was passing around a startlingly strong lemon-scented liquid they seemed to be slathering everywhere.

"What is that? It smells gross." I scrunched my face.

Henry laughed. "Believe me, after fifteen minutes in the heat on this un-air-conditioned bus, you will be hoping they pass it around again."

Yuck. He wasn't kidding. The lamb smell was a welcome respite from my fellow travelers.

"So, you are from New York?" Henry asked.

"Yep. Born and bred. You?"

"I am from Maryland originally. But I have been living in

New York since I finished my master's eight years ago. I am also an architect. I'm working on my PhD in Architectural History at NYU. This is my fourth summer in Aphrodisias."

Ahh. A veteran. "Have you been to other digs?"

"Yes. But not in Turkey. I am working on a book with Rob Turbo about the stadium in Aphrodisias, among other things. It is one of the best-preserved in antiquity. Mainly because the ancient city was somewhat provincial, so nobody was all that interested in sacking it. Over time, the city was buried. It was only during railroad excavation earlier this century that they discovered a lot of the sculptures that once ornamented the buildings. This fueled interest in the site and ultimately led to the discovery of the monuments, etcetera."

"What made you pivot from practicing architecture to academia?"

"Rob's been the architectural history chair at NYU forever and running that side of the show on the dig for almost ten years. I took a class of his as an elective in grad school and was hooked. He and his Oxford counterpart go back to undergrad."

"Remind me of the name of the Oxford guy?" I was almost too tired to remember my own name.

"Dr. R. T. W. Talbot, affectionately known to the world as Dicky." He affected a very Monty Python British accent.

"Well then."

"Indeed."

Two hours later, the van pulled into a rest stop for gas, and all of the passengers disembarked, including the lamb, which I now saw was a goat. I was grateful for the stop. I had to pee desperately.

I waited my turn for the stall and was horrified to see what my father referred to as a "squatsky." A Turkish toilet. It looked more like a shower stall than a toilet. You had to put your feet left and right and literally squat. Low if you wanted to avoid peeing all over yourself. These were not unheard of in very old or rural European restaurants, so I had seen them before. Further, they were common all over Japan, where I had spent a summer studying architecture, so I wasn't completely clueless to the proper form. Still, they were quite gross and you almost invariably ended of peeing a little on your shoes. When I came out of the ladies' room, Henry was standing by a makeshift BBQ near the roadside, devouring a sandwich in a cloud of dust. A marvelously mustached man was making fresh pita while another filled it with unidentifiable "street meat." I was no stranger to a street fair sausage and pepper sandwich and had a stomach like iron. Still, I was remembering the story of the son of a woman my mother knew from her book club whose best friend from his semester in Israel got food poisoning from a street sandwich and nearly died. I was weighing the odds against my rumbling stomach when Henry spotted me.

"Doner kebab?"

"Nah. I'm good. Can I just get the pita?" He laughed. "Sure."

He handed me the bread and a can of juice. The picture on the can looked like a peach. The closest thing to juice I had consumed in fifteen years outside of a Cosmo was Crystal Light. I really wanted water, but didn't want to be rude.

The juice was nectarine. So sweet and delicious, and the pita was the best I'd ever tasted.

We reboarded the bus, and I finally had the chance to really give my fellow travelers a good look. They all seemed to be farmers. A bit on the shorter side or maybe just a bit stooped from hard work. I had learned this was tobacco farming country and noticed several men smoking hand-rolled cigarettes. The women looked old beyond their years. They wore scarves on their heads and loose, modest clothing. I felt suddenly very exposed in my cut-off jean shorts and sleeveless shirt. What the hell. I rolled down my window, slapped on my Jackie O's, and lit up. I would go smell to smell with this group.

It was a tight squeeze back on the van. The lady with the goat set him next to me while she claimed her window seat in the row behind me. Then she gestured for me to pass the small animal back to her. The goat looked at me. His eyes said, "Just do it." It was official. I was one of them now. Again, the lemon shit was passed around, and this time I splashed some on myself because, let's face it, I also smelled terrible. The van sped off down the dusty, one-lane highway to its destination. Geyre. Henry and I chit-chatted a bit more as we rolled on. I saw the landscape get dryer and bleaker. Occasionally, we saw a farm, or some peasants walking with a donkey, or someone sped by on a moped. Beyond that, all seemed still as we plunged further into the white heat of the afternoon.

Finally, we stopped. Two evergreen trees flanked the head of a dirt road. The van pulled to the side so people could get off. Henry tapped me.

"Ally, this is us."

He pulled back the door and hopped out, offering a hand. I quickly clapped my huge hat on my head and scrambled onto the road. Dust flew up in my face as my feet hit the ground. The light was nearly blinding, even with a patio umbrella on my head. The driver had beaten us to the rear of the vehicle and had already dumped our belongings in the dirt. He was pulling off and waving goodbye before Henry could shout "teşekkür ederim" as I desperately checked the luggage tags to make sure the North Face bag on the ground was mine. I didn't want the goat-lady to get home and be disappointed to find my size two cut-offs, J Crew sleeveless tops, and two-piece bathing suits because we had the same bag. I threw the bag on my back and plodded after Henry through the evergreen gate and down the yellow dirt road to my destiny.

I was completely wilted and panting when we came upon a large screened-in structure with picnic tables and folding chairs, which I would learn was generously referred to as the "Dining Room." It looked more like an army mess tent. Beyond it was a long, single-story wood structure with three doors. I would learn one led to an office, another a studio, and the last a small lounge with dirty old sofas and a small TV. Further was an open quad around a dirt courtyard with elevated log cabins on the left, a toilet/shower house on the far side, and the kitchen to the right. Elsewhere on the site, there was a museum complex that also housed a lab for minor restoration of found objects.

"Home sweet home," said Henry, lifting up his Orioles cap and wiping his brow.

I scanned the scene. The place looked like a cross between the shitty sleepaway camp from the movie Meatballs and an army base. An audience gawked at me from behind the screen. My glamorous sun hat and Jackie O's suddenly seemed wildly ridiculous. More suited to sipping Campari and sodas in Capri than a tour of duty with this M.A.S.H. unit. I followed Henry over to the group.

"Here at last! How are you guys doing? This is Ally, a Penn architect. This is Tanya, in restoration; Debbie, in antiquities; Simon, in survey; and Philip, another Penn architect, you know him, right? And here comes Dr. Rob Turbo, our fearless leader!"

I nodded and smiled hello to everyone. "Dr. Turbo," I said as I shook his hand.

"Rob, please," he replied, his brown eyes meeting mine as he squeezed my hand a second too long. "You guys missed lunch, but I assume you hit Emir's stand at the rest stop?"

I looked back at Henry, who was nodding yes. A landmark, apparently. "Do you guys want coffee?"

"Yes, please," I gushed. I had no idea what time it was, but I knew it was time for coffee. Perhaps I would wake up after another cup and find myself in the Turkish 'Amptons, with piss water and all.

"Sade? Orta şekerli? Çok şekerli?" Rob quizzed. Ugh, this shit again. But wait, there were only three choices this time. They all looked at me with bated breath as if my response indicated some key factor in my value as a person.

"I'm sorry, I just want the biggest, least sweet one I can get." Everyone laughed.

Apparently, Turkish coffee was typically served in tiny, single espresso portions and brewed to varying degrees of sweetness. So, you had to order it that way in advance.

"Amerikana," Rob called to a tan, dark-haired waiter who appeared from nowhere. I blushed. Everyone else called out their orders, and he disappeared. Simon Survey pulled out the seat between him and Debbie and said, "Ear-sa seat, luv." Simon Survey appeared to be English, from where, I could not say. He had a hearty build and very "English" coloring. I sheepishly took a seat between him and Debbie Antiquities and across from Philip.

"So, you made it here in one piece?" asked Philip, a little bored.

"Indeed," I replied. "How long have you been here?" He already looked a little tan.

"Two days. I was traveling around Istanbul for a week

before." He pushed a handful of sweaty, light brown hair away from his face.

"Alone?"

"Yep." Must be nice to be a man. "I'll circle back for another week before I go home."

"How about you, Debbie?" I asked.

"I got here yesterday. I traveled with my boyfriend in Greece and ferried over. We were supposed to pick up Pano, the tablet specialist, but he couldn't get his visa in time. Turks are giving him the runaround because he is a Greek national. Typical shit. It will cost him two hundred dollars and delay him a few days. No biggie." She was also already quite tanned. She was about my size and build: five-foot-two. Fit. Her medium brown hair and eyes to match gave her a slightly plain appearance, but her voice was bubbly and cheerful.

"Is your boyfriend on the dig too?"

"No. I met him on last year's dig. He is from Penn, actually. You probably know him. His name is Andrik." Oh yeah. I knew who he was. Back then, he was half of an "it-couple." He was a few years ahead of me in the program. All of the girls thought he was cute. Fuck it. He was hot. And he had the lean, athletic body of a pro-tennis player. Was he Turkish? No. I don't think so.

"Is he here?" I asked hopefully.

"No. He stayed to hang out in Greece for a while. He will come in a couple of weeks for a visit. We will travel over the break and then meet up again for the trip home." Nice. Was no one concerned about getting a job here? Who were their parents? Eventually, a legitimate cup of coffee was set in front of me. I started to feel a little relaxed. "Ally," said Debbie, "we are roommates, so when you are ready, we can get you settled in. You might want a few pointers. First, the toilets are over there." She pointed toward a row of what looked like army latrines. "You can't flush the toilet paper because of the septic system." Wait, what the what what?

"What do you do with it?" I asked, not really wanting to know.

"There are little garbage cans in each stall. They are emptied constantly. It is not too bad." I'm sure. "The showers are over there." She pointed at a shower house. "Boys separate from girls." I should hope so! "You are going to want to shower after they hose the dirt; otherwise, you get all dusty before you can get your panties on, but you have to be quick because it dries fast, you know what I mean?"

"I'm sorry, hose the dirt?" Was that code for something?

"Yeah." She giggled. "They hose down the dirt by the showers every day. Supposedly, it is meant to wet and cool the ground a bit so that we don't get filthy and sweaty again as soon as we step out of the shower. Personally, I think they are just trying to catch one of us half-naked heading for the showers." Reassuring. The dig employed a bunch of peepers. "Also, you are going to want to shake your towel out before you use it. Scorpions like to get up in there, you know what I mean?" What the fuck?

"Scorpions? Are you serious?"

"Yeah, Ally. This isn't the Upper East Side. You are in the desert now," quipped Philip, half-rolling his eyes.

"Thank you. I know that. I just didn't know there were scorpions," I stammered a bit defensively. Don't wealth shame me. You are from Westport, asshole.

"Come on. You'll be fine. It was a shock to me too. I'm from Livingston." Debbie winked.

Thank you, Debbie. Another Shebrew, I assumed. She lit a

cigarette and offered me one. Inhale, exhale. “Besides, most summers nobody gets stung.” Great.

We sat a little longer. Apparently, another Penn architect was due to arrive in a few days. Jeff Hynes. I knew him by name only. He was also a year or two ahead of me. He was on last year’s dig but had to leave one week into the season. He went for a jog off-site and was hit by a bus and had to return stateside for knee surgery. Note to self: No jogging off site. There were also a few more antiquities specialists, an admin, and the head of the British contingency, Dicky, coming from the UK. Nobody knew their ETA. This was not unusual. And then there was Kamal. He was an architect coming from Miami University. He was actually Turkish and had participated in the dig the past few summers as a way to get home for free and have a job. He was in the last year of a five-year undergraduate degree. Apparently, his parents had a beach house less than two hours away, and Kamal brought some friends from the dig home most weekends on our day off. Could this be piss-water ‘Amptons? Regardless, I would make it a point to be friends with Kamal.

“When is Kamal coming?” asked Debbie.

“Tanya said she had a letter from him before she left. What did he say?” asked Philip.

“Ee ‘ad a lot ta say. Din’ ee, Tanya?” chimed Simon teasing. Manchester. Definitely Manchester.

“What do you mean? Tanya, what’s up with Kamal?” Debbie was scooping this out. I knew these people for five minutes, and I wanted the dirt, too. Tanya looked a little pale.

“He’s married,” she whispered, her gray eyes locked on her coffee.

“What the fuck?!” shot out Debbie, practically choking on her coffee.

"Married? To who? Why? He is twenty-two!" added Philip.

"Fa fuck's sec, what the fuck e..." I don't really know what Simon said, but he obviously did not approve.

"He's married. He got married over Christmas. Her name is Lisa. She is a graduate student in music. She will not be in Turkey this summer because she has auditions or something," Tanya trailed off. "Anyway, he will be here tomorrow morning, so you can grill him at lunch. I have to check something in the lab. I'll see you all at cocktails." And with that, she was gone before anyone could respond.

There was obviously a story here. Some intrigue. There were layers here to uncover. Secrets. I needed to do a little digging myself. And there were cocktails... that was cheering.

CHAPTER 3

UNPACKING

Debbie led me across the dirt quad from the "dining room" to our bunk. There were three cots in the small cabin, each with its own set of cubbies. Okay. It was kind of like a sleepaway camp. I spent seven years at Camp Akiba in the Poconos. I could do this. I plopped my bags down on one of the shabby cots. I noticed the towel hook over my cot and remembered about the scorpions. My eyes darted around. Debbie had already chosen another cot with the hook off to the side. For now, the third was empty.

"Is anybody else coming?" I asked hopefully, nodding at the third cot. Maybe I could sleep in one bed and hang my towel over the other?

"Yes. Kat. She comes with thc Brits." Damn. "She is another antiquity specialist, sculpture specifically. Dicky relies on her completely, but I suspect she wouldn't mind finding someone else to work with on her dissertation. She was here last year and the year before and..." She paused, biting her lip. Go ahead, Debbie. Whenever you're ready. "I think she rather fancies Rob," she said with a silly, faux-British accent.

"Rob who? You mean Dr. Turbo?"

"Dr. Turbo indeed," she continued with the British accent. "His rep back in NY is that he is super hands-on, you know what I mean?" I did. "He gets on well with the grad students, and there have been rumors. Simon told me he was at Oxford for a symposium and met up with Kat 'down-a-pub,' and she told him she fancied Turbo." Okay, Debbie, enough with the accent. You sound like Eliza Doolittle. I was half waiting for a musical number.

"Wow. Well, I mean, she is a PhD student and not one of his... I could see..."

"Still, I don't think this would sit well with the University. And I am sure it wouldn't sit well with his wife." Her eyes widened. I was going to have to make a chart to track all of this. I wanted to probe her more about the Kamal/Tanya situation, but realized I desperately had to pee. Anyway, she was obviously a yenta. I was sure if I just kept my mouth shut, she would soon tell me everything.

I walked across to the outhouse building. The guys were starting to hose down the dirt. They nodded in my direction. Suddenly, I remembered the toilet paper deal and wondered if I could hold it in for seven weeks. Here we go.

When I walked out, I came face to face with Philip heading in. It was an awkward opportunity to speak to him alone. Maybe he was rushing to deal with an urgent situation and would brush me off or say whatever to get behind the door as fast as possible. Regardless, I took a chance.

"Philip. How've you been? What have you been up to since graduation?"

"Really, Ally? You picked an odd moment to play catch-up." He was either about to shit himself or just wanted to make this difficult. Still, I'm like a dog with a bone.

"Well, anyway. I just wanted to say I'm sorry and I'm hoping we can be friends... like we were... before." Awkward.

"Yeah. Sure. Whatever." He looked past me toward the toilets.

"It's just that... well, we never really talked and, no hard feelings, right? We were good friends and probably should have just left it at that, you know? And..." I was really blowing the mea culpa.

"Ally, we're good. Okay?" His eyes widened, and he was nodding toward the can. Note to self, if you ever want to have a tough conversation quickly, catch somebody on their way to the toilet.

I went back to the cabin and continued to unpack. Debbie was there writing letters, presumably to Andrik. Surprisingly, it was a good bit cooler inside than out. Even without AC. I reluctantly hung a towel on the hook over my bed. There were some flat sheets folded on the stained cot mattress. I looked over at Debbie.

"Do you know where I can get a fitted sheet? There are just two flat sheets here. And no blanket."

She snorted, "No fitted, hun. Just tuck the flat in around the mattress. And you won't need a blanket. The temperature barely drops at night." Ugh. No cool corner to jam my foot into?

The mattress was really gross. She noticed me flipping it and cautiously examining the other side.

"Don't bother. I think these mattresses were the first thing they dug up here." She snorted to herself again. "Kat claims she got scabies from hers last year. I think she got it on her own time, if you know what I mean." I knew what she meant but was still horrified. How long could scabies live in a mattress? Can you even get scabies from a mattress? If I brought some exotic bed bugs back to the US, my mother would have to be committed. This just kept getting better.

"What time are cocktails?"

"People show up at six-thirtyish on. Dinner is at seven-thirty."

"What do you do after dinner?"

"Well, people usually hang around a good bit after dinner in the dining room. Sometimes they watch soccer in the lounge. Sometimes people hang out in the ruins. They are lit at night, and it is pretty amazing. I wouldn't go alone though... you never know, know what I mean?" This time I wasn't sure I knew what she meant.

"Are there wild animals or something?"

"I wouldn't say wild," she giggled. "Although a local herd of goats has been known to wander onsite. No, I mean you might get some local guys or dig workers or something. They generally leave us alone, but sometimes... for women it's best to travel in pairs after dark." Great to be a woman. She looked out the window. "Looks like the dirt is done. Ready for a shower? If you want any hot water, best not to wait too long." She was already stepping out of her shorts. She wrapped herself in a towel and threw a smaller one over her shoulders. "Come on!"

I followed suit, grabbing my shower caddy, and we headed to the showers. She was right about the dirt crew. They were lingering with the hose near the back of the kitchen, and I could practically feel their eyes willing a sudden hurricane-force gust to rip our towels away. I gripped at mine and looked at my feet.

Despite the still ample supply of hot water, I took a cold shower. I needed to cool off and wake up. It was weird. Even though the men were separated from the women by a corrugated Plexiglass partition that sat on top of an almost six-foot plywood wood panel wall, I could still see the tops of their heads and their feet. I felt very exposed and wondered if someone much taller than I could see a lot more on our side. Luckily, it was just Henry in there, and he barely had three inches on me.

By the time we were heading back to the cabin, the dirt was pretty dry, and I was already flip-flopping dust up all over myself. I started to dress, and Debbie suggested I spray on bug repellent before I put on clothes. "Even though it is so dry here, mosquitoes will still get ya." I looked at my scabies mattress and thought repellent couldn't be a bad idea. I donned a fresh pair of cutoffs and a tee shirt that barely reached the fly. Like Rachel from Friends. It was 1998, after all. I looked over at Debbie. She had on loose pajama-like capris and a matching ¾ sleeve top. I thought of the mosquitoes and considered my wardrobe. I did not pack well. There may have been an email about this or something, but if so, I sure as hell didn't see it. I was forced to get an email address to graduate. I didn't even know it or how to check it. I really couldn't see how this would ever be useful. Silly girl.

We met up with the others just after six-thirty. The whole team seemed to have been on the email chain. Except Rob Turbo whose camo cargo shorts and matching shirt hung a bit on his wiry frame. All told, he must have had at least twenty pockets, and they all seemed to be filled with something. Without staring too long I could see a water bottle, flashlight, small sketch pad, pens, probably condoms.... He addressed the group.

"Great, we are all here now? Except Kamal and the Brits, of course. And Simon appears to be delinquent out of solidarity?"

"Ere I am. Steady. Eres the maps. Fa la'a" Really. This guy seemed nice enough, but I was going to need subtitles.

"Thank you, Simon. Yes. So we will kick off the season with a lecture tonight in the baths. Of course, I encourage you all to sniff around on your own afterwards and familiarize/re-familiarize yourself with the various monuments. Yes, even the vets. Ladies, as always, please grab a buddy in the field after dark. Tomorrow, we meet for breakfast at six-thirty in order to be in the field by seven and get in as many hours as possible before the real heat kicks in. Don't worry about an alarm. The first call to prayer is around five a.m. Although, if you are the type that falls back to sleep after that... you're on your own. We will start tomorrow AM with a talk about portholes and passages in the field. Then break into our groups and get situated. Kamal just called the office and said he would be here before lunch tomorrow, and still no word from the Brits. Everyone have a drink? Right. So, to a great season." Everyone knocked back a shot of raki. I sipped on my beer trying to unpack everything he just said. I remembered the mystery surrounding Kamal. I would make a point of digging around that later. Once I had Debbie to myself.

I noticed the group putting away the bottle of raki one shot at a time. When it was empty, everyone grabbed a beer and headed for the dining room. Well, I guess the first night was cause for celebration. I was still tired from traveling and could barely finish one beer.

Dinner was surprisingly good. There was something called kofta, which were grilled meat patties (I assumed lamb) and yummy potatoes. I was hoping a summer of hard physical work and no Tasti D would result in a slimmer me. If I got off the plane with a savage tan and five-plus pounds thinner, at least my mother would see some benefit to the endeavor. Like seven free weeks at Canyon Ranch. Better skinny and without prospects than fat.

There was fresh yogurt on the table and garlic juice meant to go on everything. I used both generously. I figured the yogurt might help stave off any parasites, and as for the garlic, well, I wasn't planning on kissing anyone.

At the table, I listened more than I talked for a change. I learned Simon had a wife and a baby boy back in Manchester he was really missing. I could tell he was kind and had a good sense of humor. Pano, the tablet guy, finally had his visa and would be timing his ferry to meet the Brits at the airport upon their arrival and deliver them to the site.

While the table was being cleared, the young guy appeared at its head with a small pad, and everyone started shouting their coffee orders again. He kept his dark head down while he scribbled. I couldn't remember which was the no-sugar and which was super sweetened...and I was afraid another Amerikan would keep me up all night, even if the heat didn't. "Is there any herbal tea?" I whispered to Philip.

"Nane çayı, lutfen!" He called out, pointing to me. I smiled, embarrassed. "It's mint tea," he said without looking at me. I was going to have to write that down.

The coffee and tea were brought out. I tasted the tea. It was good but again overly sweet. I imagined getting a hot beverage served just the way I wanted it was going to be like trying to find fat-free gelato in Florence during my semester abroad in 1992. Difficult, but doable. Another waiter came out with what looked like a pizza tray and set that down, smiling. I'm pretty sure he was the hose perv from earlier.

"Yasa!" cried Rob Turbo. "They have given us a special treat to start the season!"

I looked at Debbie. "Is that...?"

"Baklava. They almost never give it to us. They buy it in town. It is ridiculously amazing; you know what I mean?"

The baklava was oozing sweet, just like on the plane. My mouth was watering. It was cut into tiny, one-inch squares. I indulged slowly, tasting the flaky, buttery pastry and the sweet and salty nut mixture. I closed my eyes. "Baklava" must mean heaven in Turkish.

"Ya awe ite, luv?"

"Yes. Thank you, Simon." All eyes were on me. "It's just so good."

"Ave anotha. Go on. Ers plenty."

"Well, maybe one more piece." I had two more missions. First, to find a way to get regular exercise here, and second, to find a way to get regular baklava. Almost never was nowhere near enough.

We congregated with our flashlights in the ancient bath complex after dinner. The monuments may have been well lit, but the paths to get there certainly were not. I was feeling a seventy-five percent chance of a face-plant. Even in sneakers.

It was pretty incredible. I had traveled throughout Europe and Asia and even Australia. I had been back and forth across the US twice. Still, I had never seen anything like it.

Turbo stood in front of us, clearly in his element. "As we all know, while the ancient inhabitants of Aphrodisias were ethnically Greek, the city, like all of Asia Minor at that time, was ruled by the Roman Empire. Hadrian, the Roman Emperor, came to Aphrodisias during one of his travels in Anatolia. The city council had commissioned these baths in memory of this visit. The bath complex consisted of two large sections, one for men, one for women, who washed separately. There was a pool with marble columns at the corners, in front of the entrance on the northern side. There were dressing rooms (apodyteria), a cold room (frigidarium), and a warm room. Under the structure, a complex of galleries and corridors made up the heating system, called the hypocaust. Throughout the structure, sandstone was used, and it was covered with marble slabs. In the front yard of the building (palaestra), was a very ornate section where Eros, human, and animal figures were depicted in marble among acanthus leaves. This was a common characteristic of Aphrodisias School."

"These baths, while quite well-preserved, were not particularly noteworthy in their time. However, given Aphrodisias' proximity to the marble source and reputation as a center for sculpture production for the Eastern Empire, the sculpture is of particular interest. When we visit Ephesus, we will compare the relative lack of sophistication of the work here. Feel free to look around; watch your step," he concluded. I sat on a wall, my short legs dangling for a while, looking around me, contemplating this Cleveland, Ohio, of the ancient world. I could hear a call to prayer from the village. It was pretty loud. I knew the sound traveled better in the dark and wondered what time was the "last call," so to speak. Suddenly feeling the weight of my travels, I wanted to go back to camp and crash. The others chatted in pairs and walked around the ruin complex. I was summoning the courage to ask for an escort when Tanya plopped down next to me. She must have had six inches on me because her feet touched the ground.

"You look done. Enough for one day?"

I laughed. "That obvious? It's been an endless day. I think it is afternoon in New York or maybe tomorrow morning? I've lost track."

"I'll walk back with you," she offered, running a hand

through her chin-length dark bob. "I've had enough of today, too."

We said our goodbyes to the crew and headed back together, making small talk. She was originally from Connecticut and was completing her PhD in restoration. She had been to digs in Egypt and Greece and had even spent part of the spring semester assisting the group restoring the frescoes in Assisi, Italy, after the devastating quake the previous September. I remembered these frescoes from my travels. They were painted by Giotto in the thirteenth century and marked a pivotal period in late medieval/pre-Renaissance painting. How amazing to be able to touch history so directly. I guess I was part of this club now. I was starting to feel better. Soon we were back at camp. I went my way, and Tanya hers. I watched her lanky frame disappear into the dark and bolted up the stairs of my cabin.

Washed and brushed, I reluctantly lay down on my cot. Despite the heat and the yuck, I drifted off almost immediately.

Midnight. Last call was midnight... or almost. It shook me from a weird dream. My father was dressed from head to toe in white sheets with one on his head tied with a bandana. With his salt-and-pepper beard and dark glasses, he looked like a bad eighties movie excuse for a Saudi oil prince. He was trying to sell me to some guy for a pile of cash and a 1980s-sized Mercedes 300SEL. However, there was heated negotiation because, apparently, I talk too much. He eventually unloaded me for a Toyota Camry and a tray of baklava. I really needed to skip dessert going forward.

Awake, I locked eyes with Debbie. She smiled in the moonlight and mumbled, "You'll get used to it." I groaned, rolled to my back, and stared at the ceiling.

"So I saw you were getting chummy with Tanya," she whispered.

"Yeah," I said dozily. "We walked back together. You know she was in Assisi this spring? Amazing."

"Yeah. I know," she said. "What else did she say?"

"Well, not much. Small talk really. Like where we were from and where we went to..."

"She seemed really bothered by Kamal's situation, if you know what I mean." She paused. Take your time, Debbie, but hurry up... I'm bushed. "Like annoyed or... sad."

I helped her. "Did they have a good relationship? I mean, were they particularly good friends?"

"Well, I'm not sure. I mean, I don't want to gossip or anything."

"Of course!"

"But I think they kind of had a thing, if you know what I mean." There you go. "And I just wonder, what's going to happen now? He is married and everything. You know what I..."

Thank you, Debbie. Yes. I wondered that too as I drifted off for the night.

CHAPTER 4

THE BEGINNING

I dreamed again. This time I was in the army. I think I was Private Benjamin and about to marry the French gyno, except he was a lawyer... and I think it was JFK Jr. Then suddenly I heard a horn and some words I didn't understand, and the rabbi was dressed like Aladdin and looked like the creepy hose guy... and I was awake. Five a.m. First call to prayer. I was seriously jet-lagged or maybe having an insulin coma from all of the baklava. Debbie was looking at her watch and setting a snooze. I rolled over and drifted back to sleep.

The alarm went off, and it was time to get up for real. The light was still dim outside, which was good because a bright light might have given me a stroke. We dressed and staggered out onto the dirt field just as the rest of the crew started to crawl out of their cabins and make their way to the bathrooms. We looked like the lone survivors of an apocalypse searching blindly through the dust cloud at the end of the world.

We congregated at the table a little later. This time the coffee was in pots already on the table. Thank God. I only hoped it wasn't pre-sweetened... but I decided to take my hurdles one at a time. The group was dressed in lightweight shirts and pants that covered way more of their skin than my cut-offs and fitted "Everlast" tank. Either these guys were total tan amateurs, or I was a desert heat dummy. The boob sweat already accumulating around my torso before seven a.m. hinted at the latter. Yikes.

Also on the table were bread and butter, fresh apricots, and some kind of cheese. "What kind of cheese is this?" I asked.

"White," everyone responded and laughed. Nobody knew its name, and it tasted like mild feta. The apricots were so sweet it was like spreading fresh jam on the bread. Added to the salty cheese, it made a delish breakfast sandwich. I think I drank six cups of coffee. It was not sweetened, thankfully, but the cups were small. I could have downed more, but didn't want to be rude. Besides, Turkish coffee was strong. I didn't want to have a poop emergency in the field, even though I was pretty sure the toilet paper situation would lock my system up tight for all seven weeks.

It was already very hot when we headed out as a group to the tetrapylon, or monumental gateway. It is a type of ancient Roman monument of cubic shape, with a gate on each of the four sides, generally built on a crossroads. Turbo started to talk about the restorations over the last century and how as the monuments were excavated, they were generally reassembled and restored with bits and pieces meant to imitate the original. The result was kind of tacky, if not sometimes misleading and inaccurate. The more recent trend was to fill in the missing parts with enough placeholders and connections made of plain concrete or other neutral material not meant to resemble original work. With this technique, you could easily tell old from new as well as the state of what remained of the original. It was more authentic and honest. These "ghost parts" also left a little more to the imagination. I could see the difference and agreed.

Next we explored the Temple of Aphrodite beyond the gate. The temple had been dismantled and reconfigured as a Christian basilica in the early centuries of the first millennium. What remained of the original temple now was basically columns. You could see the foundation blocks that made the footprint of the structure though.

We had a short break to pee and rehydrate before dividing into our smaller groups.

Henry was the leader of mine. He and I, along with Jeff Hynes when he arrived, would be using a theodolite to map tracks of land identified as possible future dig sites. Based on what they knew of the city plan from any historical accounts, plus what they could infer from typical Roman cities in the region from that time, they could anticipate where certain building types or pieces of buildings might be. The theodolite would measure the horizontal distance between two points as well as the vertical. The starting point was already mapped in relation to a known and documented point. This information could create a topographical field map of a piece of land in relation to, for example, the temple where the historians believed important sculptures or articles might be buried. Additionally, this map would be an underlayment to further develop the city plan. Then the survey team would use a device that employed a type of ultrasound and painstakingly cover every foot of our mapped plot, divided into a grid, to find anomalies in the soil that suggest something buried. Once they had plotted the location of these anomalies, they could analyze if the patterns indicated a possible monument or other structure of note. Additionally, the architecture team would be working one-on-one with an archeologist to document the bits of structures that had already been excavated. To do so, we had to stand in the field on a wall or in a ditch and sketch every stone to scale. Some of these would be partially or completely reburied to protect them after they had been recorded and used to piece together the entire city plan. That was Turbo's baby, and the project he was working on with Henry. It was cool to think I was playing a part in research that would be published, and perhaps even parts or the whole of my drawings might be included.

We dragged the theodolite case up a hill and started to unpack it. Henry set up the tripod and showed me how to level it using the plumb bob. Next he showed me how to capture the location once another team member took the pole with the target to that point. He stood fifty feet away to let me do it. Then we switched so I could see the other end. We started to survey the points one by one. It was a slow start until I got the hang of it. The device had to be readjusted with every new point. But eventually it went faster, and we chatted about this and that as we worked. Soon it was almost noon, so we packed up the equipment and headed back to camp. It was hell hot, and I welcomed the break. My almost black hair was burning to the touch. I made a point to remember my Penn cap before heading back out.

Some people had already congregated in the dining room and were whispering amongst themselves. They stopped when they saw us and looked up guiltily. Apparently, Kamal and Jeff had arrived and were unpacking. They would join us for lunch so I would be working on Debbie for details during the "rest hour" before we headed out again. I joined the others and soon everyone trickled in, including the mysterious Kamal. He was very cute. He wasn't tall, maybe five-foot-nine, with an olive complexion that was already tan. His hair was like mine, almost black and more straight than wavy. It was neatly cut but long enough on top to necessitate a fairly regular sexy shake away from his eyes... which were a beautiful hazel green. He did look young though. He was just about twenty-two, and I was twenty-six... and a half. Not my thing. Also, given the tense Philip situation, I was best off keeping my nose clean. I didn't need to give Philip a reason to spill dirt about me... assuming he hadn't already. And of course, Kamal was married. Still, meow.

Everyone was getting reacquainted and catching up as we all took our seats. Tanya hadn't appeared yet. I waited for an introduction. Finally, there was a pause in the conversation, and he looked my way.

"Hi. I'm Kamal, an architect."

"Hi, Ally, also an architect."

"Nice to meet you, Ally. You are from Penn, yes? Like Jeff and Philip?"

Damn.... Had Philip already talked shit about me, or was he just assuming I was from Penn because the other architects were? Whatever. "Yes. I just graduated. And you?" Like I didn't already know.

"Miami University."

"Ah, so you concocted a plan to escape the heat for the summer and decided to come here?" Really, his eyes were devastating, and somehow he was still clean enough to smell good.

"Exactly," he laughed. "Actually, my parents live about two hours from here on the beach, so I am near home, without being home. It is convenient for days off." Tell me something I don't already know, Kamal. He was very personable. Not too cocky. His English was flawless. I noticed all other conversations had stopped and the group was fixed on our exchange. I smiled his way and turned to the crowd.

"So, what is for lunch today?"

"Am I late?" A voice called from outside the mess. All eyes turned toward Tanya. She looked put together. No make-up, but her hair was down, and she was clean. I swear this was like a sweaty, shit-clothes Melrose Place. It was dead silent, and then the afternoon call for prayer broke the ice.

"Hi, Tanya."

Kamal got up and gave her a big hug. It was so tense. God, this was almost as good as the baklava, and no less sticky! Perfectly, at that moment hose perv and the other guy swept in carrying trays. The whole crowd turned their way in unison.... Was it time for a commercial break? I hoped not.

"Ah, pasta with Bolognese," said Philip rubbing his hands together.

"My favorite," Debbie chimed in.

The staff put a bowl in front of each of us, the napkins and flatware already on the table. There was also more yogurt and garlic. A little heavy for lunch in this heat, but what the hell. I had schlepped that freakin' heavy theodolite all morning in the heat. I dug in. The silence was a little uncomfortable. Throughout my life, I have often been accused of talking too much, specifically in awkward moments when the silence is crushing. I subconsciously need to fill the space with my voice, and sometimes I sound ridiculous and feel like a dancing monkey desperately trying to lessen the intensity of a moment. So, naturally, I asked, "Is it lamb?"

"Yes!" The group chorused. Slowly, everyone started to relax, and the chit-chat started up again. Kamal was the center of the conversation, which was a relief. I could relax and listen and not have to worry about being "on." I watched Tanya throughout the meal, looking fidgety and uncomfortable. The Bolognese was delicious. I felt ready to pass out when the coffee thing started up again. Oy. I think I must have actually said, "OY!" because Kamal looked at me and laughed and asked, "What's wrong with Turkish coffee?"

"Nothing," I said. "I just can't remember how to order it with no sugar." I scrunched my nose.

"Orta," he called and gestured to us both. Humm... we were coffee twins. Good start, Ally.... Hose perv's comrade nodded and returned to the kitchen. There were almond biscuits on the table with the coffee. We all sat and chatted a bit. When I saw Debbie get up and head for our bunk, I practically chased her.

She flopped down on her bed and stared at the ceiling. I pretended to be engrossed in a novel. Whenever you're ready, Debbie....

"So, Kamal is cute, right?"

I pretended to be so into my book that I didn't hear her. "What, sorry?"

"Kamal, he's cute, right?"

"Uh, yeah. He seems nice." She needed a little push.

"Yeah. Sure. He is super nice. And cute, right?"

I pretended to think about it. "Um. Sure. Yeah. And he seems friendly, too."

"Very friendly, if you know what I mean." She looked at me with raised eyebrows and paused as if considering whether to go on. "In fact, before Andrik and I got together, I mean we really didn't get together until the very end last year. And before, I kind of had a little crush on Kamal." She was practically whispering. I put down my book.

"Really?" I asked with interest.

"Yes." She sat up and crossed her legs, like I was her

confessor, and she let loose after barely taking a breath. "You see it was before he met Tanya. She was at Ephesus the first three to four weeks or so. Kamal and I, we were kind of hanging out, if you know what I mean. I even went to his parents' house and met them on our day off." Don't get ahead of your skis, Debbie, I already know everyone goes at some point. "But he is like five years younger than me. I mean I'm a PhD candidate, and he is an undergrad. Could you imagine? Anyway, I put the brakes on it before he got too serious and said we should just be friends." Sure, Debs. "And then Tanya came a week later and before long it looked like those two were getting chummy, if you know what I mean."

"So, they were a couple and now she is bumming because he got married over the winter?"

"Well, no. I mean yeah. We all knew they were messing around, but they never acknowledged it. I mean he is more than six years younger than she is. But she liked him a lot for sure. Did you see her face at lunch? Like a deer in headlights. She was talking to me this morning about him and wondering out loud what his deal was. Like if it was a real marriage, you know what I mean?"

"Wow," I said. I wanted her to feel I was impressed with the load she just dumped on me. And I was. But still, I wanted a little more. "So how did you and Andrik get together?"

As I mentioned, Andrik had had a girlfriend at school before: Nina. She was well-liked and very pretty in the annoying, natural French way. I knew it was a stormy on-again, off-again situation, and I was genuinely interested in how Debbie snagged him on an off swing. He was kind of a hottie and, not to be a bitch, Debbie was a little plain, empirically. She was bright and interesting, bubbly and sweet, but since when do guys go for the nice girl? Plus, Andrik had the reputation of being a player and kind of an asshole. Nina was known to have him wrapped around her finger. However, occasionally his adoration of her got boring, and she pushed him aside. He would then fuck his way through the Graduate School of Fine Arts to prove how desirable he was, and ultimately, they'd get back together. It was a little toxic, but who was I to judge? The girls he graced with his attention were always stunning. He had his pick of admirers on the back burner. So why Debbie? Had Andrik matured? Did men do that? Hmm....

"Oh, I was here all last summer, and well, Andrik didn't come until the last few weeks. After the break. Really more to help Rob specifically, but oh shit. It is one-thirty. I've got to get back to my hole in the ground. Let's go." The wily minx was out the door, but we'd catch up later. I looked around for my cap and spied it on the hook over my towel. Not having the nerve to touch it, I grabbed my ridiculous sunhat from my bed and headed for the mess to meet up with Henry.

The purpose of the break was to hide out during the worst of the heat, but really it was like an oven anyway. We dragged the theodolite to another location and started surveying a series of points from that spot. I had the pleasure of skipping from here to there with the target while Henry had me in the crosshairs. The time alone gave me the opportunity to decompress and get into my thoughts.

Graduate school was three years of merciless grind. Architects are expected to pull all-nighters, or "charrettes," regularly to make deadlines for presentations or reviews. You are constantly criticized on your ideas and execution. The studio environment can be a relentless rat race of competition, backstabbing, and toxic relationships, romantic, platonic, and academic.

This is only exacerbated by the fact that for most of us, our main associations were with other architecture students. Partially because of the unforgiving hours we kept, but also because we existed in a pseudo-intellectual bubble of like-minded Kool-Aid drinkers validating each other and enabling our inability to communicate or relate with anyone else entirely. Sounds fun, no?

This wasn't true for some. There were a few married and/or older students, with a reason to leave the studio, who managed a more normal life. But for most of us, we were on a loop of up too late, smoking too much, eating like crap, and feeding off each other's insecurity, frustration, and isolation that seemed to circulate through the architecture building more effectively than the heat or AC.

I felt all of this in spades. As an undergraduate business major, I was already years behind the others in terms of experience and understanding the nature of this cult. I kind of had my ass handed to me for at least the first year and a half, if I am being honest. I was far from the golden child I had been in school up to that moment. I clawed my way up for three years and prevailed in the end by being nominated for the coveted "thesis prize," the award for best graduate thesis project. I went home for Mother's Day the day before the nominated project presentations were to occur, only to find my entire project stolen upon my return. No shit. All of the drawings. A year's work. My thesis advisor, practically in tears, called the police. I stood in the studio giving my statement, about to burst out laughing. The message was clear. No. You cannot slack. You must remain vigilant. Nobody is rooting for you or coming to save you. Ally, my dear, you are on your own. Luckily, I had the drawings documented as they were completed so I had something to put in my portfolio, but the originals were all gone.

I swore to myself at this moment I would have to find a way to do this thing and exist in this world of imagining and making that I loved so much without being completely ruined. All of that said, it was one of the most important periods of my life. Although I emerged not knowing one hundred percent the path I would take, I knew for sure what I wanted to avoid. I would need grit and the tenacity of a Pitbull. Nobody could tell me "no," although plenty had tried.

First, the female career advisor at Penn told me architecture was not a "good career for a woman." Really. At fuckin' Penn! Based on this kind of bias, I wondered what career would be good for a woman. Silly girl.

My parents were no more supportive. When I announced in February of my sophomore year that I would not be spending the next term at the London School of Economics as planned and would instead be studying art history and architecture in Florence and, oh yeah, I was going to be an architect, my parents looked at me in shock as if I had told them I was shaving my head or joining a cult in Waco. My mother called the rabbi.

My Dad literally said, "Ally, my dear. How can you be an architect? I don't know any. How will you get a job?" in a tone one would use speaking to an idiot. My sister had followed him into the practice of law. While she worked extremely hard for her success, there was no question his help had set her on this path. He really didn't think we were competent without his involvement. I had pushed my whole life to prove him wrong. I excelled at school, sought challenging and unique adventures wherever I could, and hustled for my own opportunities.

Despite all of this, there was never a word of praise or

advice regarding tenacity, networking, etc. Looking back, I see I had already done some pretty amazing things, yet I still felt foolish, incapable, and insecure.

So here I was now reflecting on all of that and licking my wounds halfway around the world. Meanwhile, back in NYC, my brand-new niece was struggling to hold up her head and sleep the night. I feel you, girl.

CHAPTER 5

ALL TOGETHER NOW

By the time we returned to camp for teatime, the hive was buzzing. Though he had arrived earlier with Kamal, Jeff Hynes skipped lunch to unpack and rest. Coffee was on the table in pots, and despite the heat, I needed it desperately.

Tanya sat next to Kamal, looking glum as he chatted with Debbie about her break plans to travel with Andrik to the east coast. He was giving some recommendations.

Suddenly, Jeff busted through the mesh and cheerily boomed, "What's up, people?" He poured himself a cup and sat down across from me.

"I know you; Ally, right? Hey, Philip." He nodded and winked at Philip across that table.

Asshole. He looked back at me. "You hang with Garcia, right?"

Julien Garcia was a student from my year in the program. He was a good bit older than the rest of us, married, and had many years of practical experience in the field. On top of that, he was a great talent and a truly good person. Like a unicorn and a rainbow. He helped me so much in my first term. We had the same critic, who was literally like Severus Snape from Harry

Potter, before you found out he was a good guy at the end—spoiler alert if you have been under a rock since 2007. Terrifying. We remained good friends throughout our coursework. Jules was very well liked and respected within the program, and being his pal gave you some street cred. He was also extremely supportive of me. Like a big brother sent there to bolster my non-existent confidence. And he was a guy I could talk to and hang out with who wasn't trying to get in my pants.

Jeff apparently was done interrogating me and looked at Kamal.

"What's up, man? Back I see." He nodded toward Tanya and smirked. She looked like she was going to vomit.

"Ima dadae now, Jeff. Come 'ere an 'ava luke, mate." Nice save, Simon.

"What? No way. Wow, man." Jeff leaned his sweaty blond head toward Simon and gave his pictures a perfunctory glance, buying enough time for conversation to shift.

"Ally, how was your first day out?" Kamal asked me.

"Hot. But really interesting. I got to see a good bit of the site."

"You know the best way to see it is running." I laughed at the thought of jogging in this heat. "No, really. We have a little group. We head out at around six when it cools off. Depending on your distance and speed, you might be late or miss cocktails altogether, but it's a good time to go. Learn your way around and then go off on your own if you like."

Well, I was looking for a way to exercise. And while I doubted I could keep up with him, the thought of chasing Kamal around the site for a while perked me right up.... Ally, you naughty girl.

"Okay. Are you guys going today?" Kamal first looked at

Tanya, who looked like she was about to combust, and nodded back to me. Great. This was the little group. I am sure I was welcome.

"Perfect. Well, I'm going to go change and cool off a bit before we go." I wasn't in the mood for drama. I went to the bathroom and rinsed my face, eyeing hose perv peeking at me from the kitchen. I changed and met the "group" at the mess at six o' clock. I had my yellow waterproof Walkman in hand, loaded with a Diggable Planets tape. Kamal and Tanya had no devices. Ugh, talkers. Even if I could keep up with them in the heat, trying to speak would kill me for sure. Damn Dunhills.

My companions started out with some light stretching, and I joined in with some very clumsy lunges. Tanya was almost Kamal's height. She bent in half over her long legs, with her ass in his direction, grabbing the backs of her ankles. I shot Kamal a raised eyebrow, and he stifled a laugh.

We started out together and before long rounded the baths we had seen last night and headed toward the stadium. The stadium at Aphrodisias was perhaps the best preserved in antiquity, if not the most refined. Kamal started running up and down the bleachers-like benches Rocky-style, and Tanya tried to keep up. No way. I walked the stairs huffing and puffing, clutching my side and regretting all of the cigarettes and coffee I'd ever consumed. Next we headed for the forum. They ran side by side discussing the state of some wine vessels Tanya was restoring. I held back five to ten feet and pretended to listen to my music, struggling to keep up while eavesdropping. Kamal was right. The ruins were amazing in the late-day light, and jogging you could experience the ancient city moving relatively quickly from one monument to the next. I felt privileged to be able to see them this way.

Finally, the mess was in sight. Beet-red and gasping for breath, I hustled to the showers. The dirt was already dry when I emerged, still sweating. Having missed cocktails, I rushed to join the others at the dining table.

The group was engaged in speculation regarding the arrival of the Brits. Evidently, they brought a fair share of their own drama. I noticed another spent bottle of raki on the table, which was already littered with empty beer cans. I could see I needed to catch up on more than the conversation. I plopped down between Tanya and Debbie who leaned in whispering about Kat. I realized I had to strain to hear any of the chat because there was a loud unmuffled motor running in the distance. Hose perv and company set plates of karniyarik, eggplant boats filled with lamb and veggies, in front of each of the crew. Very tasty, and while I suspected it was not the best version of this meal, it was still pretty good.

I was thirsty from the run and guzzling water when I realized the motor was increasing in volume. And the smell! No one seemed to notice; they were just chatting away and shouting over the noise.

Suddenly it was deafening like thunder, and a smoke cloud of exhaust filled the open-air dining room. I was on my feet, holding my plate, ready to dash for cover, but I was suddenly blinded by the smog. Oh My God! We were about to be engulfed in toxic gas! Or crop dusting or Agent Orange or some form of chemical warfare prohibited by the UN! When the haze cleared a bit, I could see the others calmly sitting at the table, looking at me like I was mad.

"What the fuck?" I shouted. "I think we've been gassed!" They were all laughing.

"It's petrol, luv. Ees burn'in it against a masqui'os," my eyes darted around. Had Simon had a seizure, or was he saying something?

Rob Turbo caught his breath. "They burn diesel to kill the mosquitoes."

"While we *eat*?" I think I was shouting now. He raised his eyebrows as if to consider for the first time the wisdom of performing the fumigation while we ate. Everyone went back to their dinner, so I sat down and did the same. Desperately in need of good news, I turned to Debbie.

"Do you think there is baklava tonight?"

"Oh no. Two days in a row? I told you almost never."

"Kamal?" I asked. "How do you ask if there is baklava?" I could see the kitchen staff shuffling about and stealing glances our way.

"Do you want me to ask?"

"No. Thanks. I just want to know how to ask myself." I had an idea that might turn almost never into a more regular deal.

"Baklava var mı?" he said, smiling.

Some of us hung around for another hour after dinner over our coffee. I sat off to the side, half trying to read a book. Debbie went back to the bunk to write a letter. Jeff started to dish as soon as she was out of earshot.

"Andrik and Debs are still a thing? I hear he is coming next week and then buzzing around half the season. I saw Nina in NYC last week, and she is still salty about it."

"I guess," replied Philip, trying not to gossip. He paused. "I haven't seen her since the end of last summer when we got back and, well. You know. She was shocked." I guess he wasn't trying that hard.

"I bet she was. Everyone was talking about it. She found out from Kat before Andrik even got back. She was furious and humiliated. They had a big blowout. He even quit his job because they worked in the same place, you know." Yikes. I wanted to get up and slink back to my bunk. I was pretty sure if they noticed me leaving, I would be next on the chopping block. I saw Tanya and Kamal in a dark corner between two buildings, but pretended not to notice. Body language told me it was an unpleasant chat, and they took two steps away from each other when they saw me. Next I heard Rob Turbo on the field telephone having an argument with someone.

I thought it was one of the Brits as the subject of their arrival came up, but I soon realized it was likely his wife. I thought about what Debbie said Simon said Kat had told him about Rob being really "friendly" with students. Shit, land mines everywhere tonight.

Once inside the bunk, I quietly slipped into bed without even brushing my teeth. I wanted to avoid any more intrigue. Luckily, Debbie was already asleep—at least pretending to be. I closed my eyes and thought about my best friend, Melanie.

Mel had just finished medical school in NYC, as I was wrapping up in Philly. The four years we spent since graduating college were tough on us both. We were inseparable since bonding over a Bobbi Brown Rum Raisin lip gloss at a frat semi-formal at the end of our first semester of freshman year. We were together every day, and although our academic interests could not have been more divergent, we were of the same mind on almost everything else. We had an endless repertoire of inside jokes and references that made it unnecessary for us to communicate in full sentences, which was good because we were giggling incomprehensibly like idiots after three words anyway. It was so empowering to know we had each other's backs. No matter what. We bolstered each other's strength and confidence, but apart we were both struggling. So many of our worries, so much of our futures were hashed out over so many cigarettes smoked on the roof of our house looking over the Philly skyline.

Together we were strong. Apart we both looked for footing on less than stable ground and often landed on our asses. Hard. It almost killed Mel, who had suffered painfully from anorexia or work-out bulimia or whatever; we never really named it. Like good Gen X-ers, we shoved it down and kept working and moving forward. I saw her put all of her hopes and dreams in the hands of a careless, self-indulgent prick who could never give her what she wanted or, for that matter, deserved. I saw her desperately trying to shake off her parents' yoke of convention by tethering herself to a man who would not be tethered. I saw her relentlessly trying to conform to a mold she thought he would deem worthy and literally and figuratively almost disappear in the process.

I remembered my parents asking me if she had cancer at my sister's wedding. She was that thin. My guilt was unbearable at times. I could not be there for her in body and spirit the way she needed me as I was being devoured by my own reality. Now I was returning to the promised land, and she was off to residency in DC. Another four years apart. At least she was leaving *him* behind. Tears welled in my eyes as I thought of Mel and drifted off to a dreamless sleep. Small mercies.

The next day was much the same until lunchtime. When Henry and I rolled the theodolite case back to camp, we heard the big news. The British were coming, and they would be arriving by tea the next day. Figures. Also, one of the local farmers had lost a goat a few days ago, so if we saw one, we should notify Turbo immediately. The locals were a little suspicious of us to begin with and probably suspected us of pinching it, so if we could assist in its safe return, it would help. Like what the hell were we going to do with the goat?

We headed back out to a new site after lunch. Again, the heat was appalling. On the way up the hill, we passed Debbie standing on a wall with a clipboard shouting to the digging crew in Turkish. She sported a billowy long-sleeved shirt, gloves, and a pillowcase strapped to her head with a purple bandana. I was impressed. She looked bad ass. I looked down at my own outfit and felt like a sorority girl on spring break in Cancun. Too much skin. And I think I smelled God awful. Or maybe it was Henry? Or ughhhh! We found the goat.

We must have seriously been upwind of this thing to have not smelled it sooner. The poor goat had fallen into an old, forgotten hole that was made when the team was spot digging to uncover an anomaly found during survey, hoping it was a building corner or some other promising point to start a major excavation. It had probably been dead for a few days. I immediately threw up on my shoes. Henry grabbed me and pulled me away, chuckling a bit.

"You okay?" I was bent over with my hands on my knees, shaking near collapse.

"Oh God. Oh my God. Holy shit." I was crying, I think, and felt very dizzy. The heat, the stench. This was too much. Henry practically carried me, or at least dragged me, back to camp and put me in a chair at the table. I could hear him speaking in Turkish to the kitchen staff and then explaining the situation to Turbo, whom he bumped into on his way back to the table. I had my head in my hands and was looking down, trying to keep from passing out. Trying to focus on the dusty puke covering my shoes. All I could see was the decomposing goat. Someone put a tall glass in front of me filled with white liquid. Were they kidding? Milk? I think I gagged again.

"Ally," said Henry, putting a cool, wet towel on my neck, "take a sip of this. Sip it down slowly. Can you hear me?"

"Ew. No. I couldn't," I panted.

"Ally, please. It is watered-down yogurt with a little salt and ice. You are dehydrated. This will help and settle your stomach."

I took a sip. It wasn't bad. I took another and actually felt a little refreshed. I sat up a little.

"There she is. I swear this shit can cure cancer. Drink it slowly. You'll be fine," Henry said, making sure I had both hands on the glass. Turbo laughed a bit and walked away, hopefully to tell someone to take care of that poor thing and bury, or even better, burn it.

"Henry, that was the most disgusting—"

"I know," he interrupted. "It happens every year. Something turns up dead and stinks up the place. Usually, we smell it sooner, so it doesn't get that bad. You should give me your shoes. I'll hose them down." Henry was a mensch.

"Thank you. Really," I whispered between sips.

I sat there, coming back to myself, embarrassed over the scene. What happened next made me think I was hallucinating.

A van slowly rolled into camp, practically into the mess itself. Before it could come to a full stop, the side slid back with a bang, and the passengers, or at least one of them, seemed to spill out into the dust.

"Bloody hell!" a voice from the dirt boomed. Two women jumped out, and one, a young doughy blond, attempted to help the man on the ground. The other, a lean striking brunette, casually grabbed her bags and stalked right past the mess toward the bunks without even looking back.

"Ah, sod off, Katty, bleedin' slag," the man muttered as he pulled himself to his feet. He was tall, red-faced, and wore matching khaki cargo shorts and a long-sleeved top. A mass of graying, light brown curls peeked out from his outback hat, the strap of which was lodged in his mouth. He put his nose in the air. "Right," he announced, spitting out the strap, "Aggie, get that Stilton in the fridge. I say, it smells like a bloody rotten carcass." He noticed me clutching my cocktail and squinting his way in disbelief. He staggered in my direction as Aggie hoisted up what seemed to be a wheel of cheese and lumbered off to the kitchen.

"Oh. Hello. Who might you be, love?" He slurred a bit, trying to straighten up.

"Hello, uh, sir. I'm Ally. One of the architects." I tried to stand. He noticed my glass and laughed.

"I dare say you had too much raki last night. Ayran, nectar of the gods that is." He pointed at my glass. Apparently, this strange elixir also cured a hangover.

"No. Dead goat. I mean, I saw, smelled a dead goat, and got sick. That is what you smelled coming in. I don't think it was your cheese."

He laughed again. "Well, love, I wouldn't be too sure. Right, where's Turbo?" he boomed, and before I could answer, he staggered off toward the field office. So those were the Brits. Rather than the think tank I thought I was joining, I seemed to have fallen into an episode of Ab Fab.

I sat alone, processing the scene for a few minutes before I noticed another passenger unloading the van and walking over with a large pack on his back. It was the driver, and I had not noticed him.

"Hi. Sorry about that. Dicky makes a great first impression.

I'm Pano. Tablets, inscriptions, expert in ancient Greek, and modern Greek as well, I guess," he said, smiling and held out his hand. "You okay?" He had a Greek accent, but his English was perfect.

"Yes. Thanks. Ally, architect. Nice to meet you. Dead goat." I held up my glass. "Rumor was you were coming tomorrow?"

"Yes, well, Kat called me and said Dicky was, well, enjoying himself too much in Istanbul and asked if I would come a day early. I met them at the airport in Izmir with the van."

"Did Dicky really bring cheese from Istanbul? In this heat?"

Pano shook his head. "No. He brought it from Oxford. Don't think you can get Stilton in Istanbul. He likes it with his Port." He gestured to a wooden case sitting in the dust. "That he brought from Istanbul. Duty Free. Excuse me now, please. I want to unpack before lunch." He walked away, leaving me there in my socks, wondering what was next.

So that was the team. We were all accounted for. I had the feeling this was about to get really interesting.

CHAPTER 6

HOT ROCKS

We assembled for cocktails that night at six-thirty. Everyone was drinking and chatting, but the tension was palpable. Dicky seemed to have sobered up enough to engage in a good-natured debate with Pano over whether or not it was time for the Elgin marbles to come home to Athens. Turbo was holding court with the architects enthralled, and Kat and Tanya were whispering conspiratorially in the corner over their raki and periodically turning their matching dark bobs toward the architect pack. Like evil Olsen twins. They looked particularly refreshed, as if efforts had been made. Kat had decided to bunk with Tanya and Aggie. This left Debbie and me with a little extra space and a remote hook for my towel, so I was happy about that.

Although Aggie primarily functioned as Dicky's assistant and had accompanied him to other digs around the ancient world, it was her first tour in Turkey. Word was Turbo had hinted to Oxford that Dicky could use some "help," or really a handler, to make the most of his time and their money. Kat's role was really more academic, and she had no patience for Dicky's bullshit.

Last summer it took him an additional week to find his way from Istanbul, and he left two weeks early to join the group at Ephesus and never showed up.

We moved onto dinner, the group still snickering about my field discovery. The food was brought out, but my appetite was still stunted by earlier events. It looked like a huge drumstick sitting in a urine-colored broth. It couldn't be turkey, could it? I didn't think they ate much turkey overseas... and then I noticed everyone was looking at me.

"What is it?" I asked Debbie, my throat tightening. She paused and looked down at her bowl, holding back a smile.

"Goat shank." Give me a fuckin' break!

I decided to pass, picking at some yogurt and taking mental notes. So, the Oxford bigwig was a drunk. Debbie was hot and heavy with Andrik but may have had a spiritual, if not physical, fling last summer with Kamal. Tanya definitely got down with Kamal last summer. She was still holding a torch despite the fact that he was now married. Kat allegedly had hot pants for Turbo, who was also married. I noticed him sitting next to Aggie. He sat back in his chair and had his arm casually draped over the back of hers. He was leaning in too closely and pointing at notes she had made on a pad. She, by contrast, sat up straight and primly. Kat stared daggers at her from across the table. Jeff was prattling on to Philip about some architect he knew at Ephesus who was "totally hot for him." He was planning to "move on" her when our group visited the site next week. Pig.

As I finished my analysis of the crew, Dicky stalked in from the office. "I say, is there someone called Ally here?"

"Yes, I am Ally."

"Right, well there are two very agitated Americans shouting into the phone. I cannot tell you what about, but it apparently involves you." He breezed past me and took his seat.

I was beet-red as I moved toward the office to answer the phone. Hose perv stood by the door and, almost as embarrassed, jumped out of my way. I was gripped with fear. Was my dad dead? Did something happen to my niece? I grabbed the phone.

"Hello? Hello!"

"Ally, Oh my God. Are you okay? Oh my God." My parents sounded unhinged and breathless.

"Mom? Dad? I am fine. Are you guys okay? You sound hysterical."

"Don't be cute. We thought you were trapped under a pile of rubble or carried off in a tsunami. Why didn't you call us? Do you think we want to hear this kind of terrifying news from Irene or Meryl?" My sister's mother-in-law and my mom's best friend, respectively. "Daddy called Bob and Jo," (recent ex-Attorney General of New York and Jewish Senator from Connecticut, respectively) "to get in with the State Department. He is on the phone with them now. Don't worry, pussy cat. Daddy will get a chopper to get you out of there if he has to." I am not even going to explain how my parents knew these people, but if you have ever heard the term "Jewish Geography," you will understand.

"What the hell are you talking about? Why am I leaving? What happened?"

"Ally, wake up! I swear you are a fart in a blizzard!" My father had a way with words.

"Howard, darling, please. Pussy cat, there was an earthquake. Six-point-three on the Richter scale in Turkey. Over a hundred dead, buildings collapsed. Wait, hold on. I'm getting another call. It's Ela Mizrahi, from my art group.... They are on with the Turkish consulate, I called her...."

"Excuse me," I was getting pissed. Why did they still assume I was helpless and hapless? "I haven't heard anything about this. It is obviously far away from here. It is not a small country. Not even a tremor here. Really."

"What? Are you sure? Howard, she says it wasn't near her. Cancel the chopper and apologize to the guy from the State Department. I think you made him cry."

"Really. I am sure. Look. I have to go.... I am missing dinner."

"Okay, doll. We love you. Call us if you need—"

I hung up and walked back to my bunk without saying "good night" to the group. I was pretty sure they were all eavesdropping on my conversation and looking for the opportunity to talk shit about me. Enjoy. It had been a long day, and my head was splitting.

I brushed my teeth and threw some cold water on my face, catching my reflection in the mirror. How did you get here, Ally? And what were you going to make of it? Historically, in my life, whenever I had shaken things up in hopes of altering its trajectory, I had been somewhat successful. Each brick I pulled from the wall of expectations built around me allowed in a little more light, at times even a space to get my foot in and see over the top. This time, I was having trouble just getting on my feet. I needed some fortification to return home for the next step. Yes, I needed a job, and not the type my parents would understand. Although I would be back in New York, I needed to put space between us. I needed something to remind myself that I had the power to take control of my destiny. Surely if the Romans could conquer most of the world known to them and erect cities without modern technology, I could stand up to P and H and live in Brooklyn with a roommate in a non-doorman building. Maybe the grandeur of Ephesus would inspire me.

Ephesus was a richer and more famous ancient city near the modern Turkish coastal town of Selcuk (pronounced Selgück) about two hours away. It was best known for its temple of Artemis, one of the wonders of the ancient world, and its importance to Christians, as John the Apostle spent years there. In the ancient world, it was like Paris, France, while Aphrodisias was like Paris, Illinois, despite the kick-ass marble quarry and well-preserved stadium. While Aphrodisias had been a manufacturing center of fine sculpture throughout the ancient Greco-Roman universe, Ephesus was a center of culture and wealth. Thus, the crew working at Ephesus was better funded, better staffed, and better equipped. While there was some coordination with the Oxford group, the Ephesus dig had been run by the Austrians for the better part of more than a hundred years. The British archeologist who began the excavations there decades before them had to abandon his work because of insufficient funding. The result was a bit of rivalry between our sites that had lasted to this day.

The days leading up to the trip followed a familiar rhythm. Wake, work, eat, gossip, and drink, drink, drink. A pitcher of ayran was now finding its way to the breakfast table daily. So many hands grabbed for it, it was impossible to determine at whose request.

I was trying to keep my head down and eyes open. It was clear Tanya was pining for Kamal. He seemed fine to maintain their relationship on a platonic basis, but was trying desperately not to raise any suspicions regarding the legitimacy of his marriage.

Kat was still uncomfortably attempting to shimmy up to Turbo. Was it boredom? Lust? Or some other motive I could not yet tell? Meanwhile, Aggie was clearly trying to get as far from him as possible.

The trip was planned for the end of the week. We would leave first thing Saturday morning to arrive onsite a couple of hours later, with a few hours to tour above ground before the worst of the heat set in.

We had been invited for a special tour of the site on Saturday, with special access not allowed to civilians. I was looking forward to it, even though we were the scrappy one-horse dig in the dust and they were the fancy city dig. This must be what people from New Jersey feel like, I thought.

We planned to spend the night as a group and the next day hit the beach at what I hoped was a "piss water 'Amptons." We were caravanning in two minivans, with Kamal following in his car. He would join us for the tour and then jump home for the night.

I was really looking forward to a "night out." I wanted to shower and maybe put on some makeup and not be filthy again before I sat down to eat. I wanted to eat in a restaurant and not be gassed in the process. And most of all, I couldn't wait to sleep on a non-scabies mattress in an air-conditioned room. Henry said you could get a room with air-conditioning for five dollars per night. Granted it was like European AC, as Howard liked to call it, which meant an inside temperature of seventy-two degrees Fahrenheit could not be achieved here until November, but I would take it. And as a bonus, we could sleep until seven-thirty, maybe eight a.m. the following day.

Finally, Saturday morning arrived. We assembled by six-thirty for breakfast and then headed out. The sky still had traces of orange and pink when we congregated at the table.

Witnessing the last moments of a spectacular sunrise was a

lot more awe-inspiring when you knew it would not be followed by a scorching day of work in the field.

I guzzled down three cups of coffee and pulled on my smoke, staring into space, still half-comatose, and listening to my colleagues gossip about the staff on the Alpha dig. Philip was wondering out loud if Gerta, the head of operations at Ephesus, would completely unravel Dicky again. Apparently, years ago when they were PhD students, they worked together on a dig in Egypt and were having an affair. It was an on-again, off-again thing for years that ultimately brought them both to Turkey. Finally, they had the chance to be together and co-run operations at Ephesus, bringing the Brits back into the fold after years exiled from the dig. Then she stabbed him in the back to push him out and take control for herself, blaming nationalist politics.

Humiliated, Dicky had to return to Oxford, having let this prize slip through his hands. To make it worse, she now had a close partner on the dig. A Frenchman called Armand. Nothing chafed the Brits like being bested by the French. Still.

Kat and Tanya were in their corner. I overheard their plan to snare Turbo into a dinner. Tanya would ditch at the last minute, leaving Kat and Turbo alone. Meanwhile, Turbo leaned lecherously over poor Aggie at the other end of the mess as she reported the day's schedule. Jeff was making lewd comments to anyone who would listen about Elsa, the "tight" architect he was looking forward to seeing, and Debbie was all a flutter because Andrik had just left a message that he would skip the a.m. tour at Ephesus but would catch up with her after for the rest of the day.

"Sorry, Ally. Looks like you are on your own tonight, if you know what I mean," Debbie chirped. She was not at all sorry. It was not even seven a.m. and already there was more Greek drama here than this place had seen in over two thousand years.

I really couldn't take much more before my coffee kicked in. I got up and walked to the lounge to grab a bottle of water for the ride, passing the kitchen where the hose perv seemed to be lying in wait for me. He startled me, so I cried out, and that seemed to scare the shit out of him. He ran back into the kitchen. It was too early to be assaulted, so I moved quickly toward the dusty driveway where the group assembled. Van one was driven by Turbo and had Kat riding shotgun, of course, with Jeff, Philip, Simon, and Debbie in tow. Van two had Pano behind the wheel, Dicky shotgun, with Aggie, Henry, and yours truly filling the back seats. Tanya lingered in the drive as Kamal pulled up behind the vans. She was obviously waiting for him to offer her a ride.

He honked and called out to Turbo. "Okay. So, I am heading out. I'll meet you guys outside the gate at ten o' clock. I'm grabbing my sister on the way." He peeled out, leaving Tanya in a cloud of dust without so much as a nod in her direction.

"Right. Tanya, do you require a personal invitation to board this vehicle?" Dicky was lucid this morning and a little testy. "Bloody hell, woman, do get in!"

Tanya sat down next to me in the back row and looked out the window, pouting. We hadn't even pulled out of the lot, and already I had major swamp ass. Sitting in the back, I figured I could stare out of the window and get lost in my surroundings and my thoughts.

We passed back through the village, and I could see the inhabitants beginning to stir. I noticed how stooped the women were and how bowlegged many of the men looked. I thought about how challenging life must be here, working the tobacco farms year after year. I imagined the loose clothing that covered both sexes from head to toe was likely explained equally by the unforgiving heat as much as modesty. I saw a young woman walking on the side of the road with one child on her hip and another holding her hand. A scarf covered her head, but I caught a glimpse of her face as we zoomed past, leaving her and her brood in a cloud of dust. Her round face was as young as mine, maybe a bit younger. This village was her past, present, and future. I was suddenly grateful for all of the choices and opportunities that I had really taken for granted. I felt guilty for not being able to maturely deal with people's expectations of me and for desiring escape and validation. Still, I cheered up as I thought of the shining promise of civilization at Ephesus.

The landscape along the almost two-hour drive was mostly arid and unremarkable. I did notice the preponderance of construction, or partial construction, along the new-looking highway. It was as if building after building was only partially constructed with additional stubs of concrete columns sprouting steel reinforcement or "rebar" left exposed. Rebar is a steel bar or mesh of steel wires used as a tension device in reinforced concrete structures to strengthen and increase tensile strength. It was as if the builders weren't committing to the final number of stories and wanted to leave their options open to expand. From what I could see, all of the construction was performed in this manner. I wondered how safe this was. It certainly wasn't pretty. Some in that state were even partially occupied.

"Henry, what happened here? It looks like these construction sites have been left unfinished."

He laughed. "Kind of. When there is money to build, they get started, optimistically leaving the door open for additional levels later on. When there is uncertainty, they take 'a break.' With the secular government in place, they are banking on joining the EU. Developers want to make sure there is infrastructure for all the new industry they are betting on."

My mind shifted back home. I didn't think this sort of cowboy construction would pass muster in even the wild world of Miami construction, forget New York. Still, there was a lot of optimism regarding the economy right now. The real estate market was booming such that you could buy an apartment and flip it in two years with barely a new coat of paint and make at least twenty-five percent on top of your investment. Interest rates were low and even dropping. There was a huge construction boom for high-end residential properties, which made my prospects for employment pretty bright. I was banking on a job with a small boutique firm I had interned with after my first year in graduate school. They had a celebrity residential and high-end retail clientele. Because it was a small operation, I could wear a lot of hats and get my feet wet in all aspects of a project long before I would see daylight in a large firm. I landed that internship on my own, though I was steered in the right direction by an incredible woman I could only describe as my mentor.

When I returned from my semester abroad junior year, I started cold calling Philadelphia architects to see if anyone needed an intern. I just wanted to get my foot in the door and see what it was about before sealing my fate. I eventually came across a Penn alumnus who had her own firm in Old City. She agreed to meet me. I remember riding my bike across town to her studio. The spring sun on my face and wind in my hair made me feel like I was flying toward my future. Even if bumping along the cobblestones and abandoned streetcar tracks meant that the future would be childless, I was doing it!

Eve Spect was a serious woman who sized me up over black-rimmed spectacles. In her studio sat three other women, all clad head to toe in black. One sat in silence, busily making a model of what looked like a house out of foam core. The other two whispered in a corner, hashing out a detail. Spect and I sat face to face on opposite sides of her enormous desk, listening to the rhythmic tap of her blood-red nails on the surface for what seemed like hours. Finally, she breathed out loudly through her nose.

"And why do you want to be an architect, Ms. Acker?"

"Well, because I am interested in building and making, and I want to address problems I believe can be solved or at least positively impacted by creating or modifying the environments where we live and work and experience our world," I sputtered. She raised a single, thin black eyebrow.

"Look, Ms. Spect, I don't know yet whether I'll spend my life renovating bathrooms or if I will ever design something that the world remembers forever. I don't care. All I think about is how to make things. And—" I choked, "I need to make them."

She leaned forward on her desk and grabbed onto my hands.

"Well, Ms. Acker, to look at you, I'd guess you wouldn't even know how to make a bed. But," she studied my fingers and looked at my palms, "these hands have clearly been working on something. And by the state of your cuticles and the stench of cigarettes coming off you, you clearly have enough angst to at least suggest an artistic temperament. I did some snooping on you." She pointed one of her red talons at my face and looked me squarely in the eyes as if she was weighing all of my flaws against my potential. "You are very clever, but that will not be enough." She practically threw my hands back at me and pushed back in her chair. "You can come here. I will find something for you to do. It will not be glamorous. You have no skills I can use. We will see what you are made of. This is not a path you should follow if you are not prepared to eat shit. And believe me, the boys will feed it to you!" She stood up and stalked to the studio door. I could see then that she was just about my height and heroine-thin. Her straight bobbed hair was so black it looked like the hood to her all-black uniform.

"I will see you Friday afternoon. You can pick up my lunch on your way. My right-hand Lou will tell you what I eat." She waved a hand toward one of the women in the corner. "Dress for some messy work but always tidy. I see clients in this studio. If working here doesn't change your mind, I may decide to help you." She looked me up and down. "You will need it." And with that, I was dismissed.

And she did help me. In addition to helping me put together my portfolio, connecting me with her photographer, and helping me select the work to include, she generated a solid list of schools for me to apply to. All the while telling me it was a long shot and not to be surprised if I got rejected from every single one. She was so proud when I got into Penn. She threw a little party for me in the studio, toasting to my future.

I went later to thank her for believing in me as well as for everything she had done to help me, and she grabbed my shoulders, looked me dead in the eyes, and said, "Of course I believed in you. You are smart and savvy and resourceful. But what I think is horseshit. Ally, my dear, you must never stop believing in yourself!" With that, she shoved a black journal and a beautiful pen in my hands. "Write down your dreams, Ally. Write them down because some days you will need to remind yourself why the fuck you are still here. Draw what inspires you because you will need the inspiration. Keep the promises you make to yourself. They are the most important ones you'll make and the first you will break. Good luck. You will need it." And just like that first day, I was dismissed.

I saw her sometimes throughout my tenure as a grad student. She would show up at a review as a critic or just to watch the fine arts students present. She did me one last solid that would again change my life. After my first year, she left a full set of the New York yellow pages for "Architects" photocopied in my school mailbox with certain firms highlighted and a Post-it that said, "Worth your efforts."

And that is how I knew where to look for a job in The City that summer and how I ended up with a solid lead on one now.

I was snapping out of my trance as the coast came into view in the distance. We were nearing Selcuk.

The minivans parked in a sliver of remaining mid-morning shade, and we all got out, leaving our overnight things to slow-cook for the day. The minute the door to the car opened, one fact was clear: Despite the proximity to the coast, somehow, it was at least ten degrees hotter here than back at our camp, and it was still early. With twenty minutes to kill until meet-up time, I ducked into a café with Henry in search of a bathroom and another bottle of water. Waiting my turn, I noticed a few young women in the streets sporting more "Western" clothing. Uncovered heads, shorts, tank tops. A few must have been international visitors like me, but even some of the tourists were likely Turkish, given the fame and popularity of the site. The café was populated mostly by men who sat in small groups, chain-smoking unfiltered cigarettes and sipping coffee from Lilliputian cups or tea from pretty glasses. It reminded me of

Italy during my semester abroad. Could one have a job in New York that required haunting a café for half the day? If so, were they hiring?

As Henry and I made our way from the café to the entrance of the site, we passed several carpet shops with the most beautiful rugs and kilims, or flat weave rugs, hung from the walls and piled on the floor. The proprietors of these shops bowed as we passed and called invitations to us to join them for tea. By the time the fifth carpet salesman bent at the waist and waved us into his carpet-clad lair, I was starting to feel they were disingenuous in their hospitality. Henry advised me to ignore them. He knew a man in town who was honest and fair, and if I was serious about a carpet, he would take me later. However, he warned me, I would be obligated to sit for tea, listen to a dozen stories about the carpets, and very possibly be introduced to his entire family. No problem, Henry. Anything for a good deal. And while a lovely handmade Turkish carpet might just be the last thing I needed on which to blow a good chunk of my "stipend," it would be the first thing I needed to furnish my new apartment in New York.

We met the others at the gates and were escorted by a very official-looking man with a clipboard and a French accent past the throngs of civilians waiting in line to enter. I assumed this was "Armand." Kamal was there with his sister. She was in her late teens and was sporting short cutoffs and a tank top with "Brooklyn" printed across her boobs. She greeted the crew members individually, and I remembered they had all been to her home at the beach at least once. She turned to me and introduced herself, smiling.

"Hi. I am called Ayeleen."

"Hi. I'm Ally."

Ayeleen was studying to be a civil engineer, like her parents, at a university close to her home. She was very cute, like her brother, and had a warm, welcoming smile. Tanya was instantly on her with a hug and a big hello.

Armand led us through the gates, and we walked as a group over the five hundred yards of colonnaded marble road. In ancient times, this road was lit up at night by oil torch streetlamps. It must have been stunning. The paving stones on the road were inscribed with graffiti, some dating from ancient times. The inscriptions indicated directions to various businesses, including a house of ill repute.

Next we moved on to the Celsus Library. This is the most iconic monument of Ephesus. It was the third largest library of the ancient world, with a capacity of twelve thousand scrolls. Even today, Celsus's sarcophagus lay in the crypt under the building. Celsus was the city's Roman governor, and the library was built in his honor by his son in the second century CE.

The ornate facade housed sculptures held in a series of niches framed by columns. The statues, which symbolized the virtues of Celsus—wisdom, knowledge, intelligence, and valor—were reproductions. The originals could be found in Vienna.

We, of course, were brought behind the velvet ropes to parts of the library only accessible to the pros, the proverbial VIP section. By the time we were back outside, one thing was clear. Ephesus must mean white-hot hell because unbelievably it was even hotter than before. Someone was muttering something about the white marble reflecting the heat and light like a mirror, but honestly, I was focusing on not passing out.

Mercifully, we headed back inside and underground to where it was a bit cooler to see some dwellings not yet open to the public that showed the tremendous wealth of the ancient city's inhabitants. There were beautiful floor mosaics and stunning wall paintings. A structure was in the works to protect these buildings from the elements, specifically the sea air. There was scaffolding to navigate, and we worked our way down. Members of the field team swarmed about shouting in German while sweating local men with wrapped heads carried out buckets of dirt. I felt like I was in an Indiana Jones movie. Like someone might open a sarcophagus and turn us all into dust.

When we popped above ground again, it was time for lunch. We were to head back to Selcuk to eat and rest and would return refreshed to the site, specifically the theater, at six-thirty for a special sunset lecture and cocktails. I hoped the temperature would drop significantly at the end of the day, or any effort to look human would be futile.

We broke into smaller groups for lunch. Debbie was already gone, off to rendezvous with Andrik. Dicky and Turbo were lunching with the other dig's top brass and had taken Pano. The rest of the Brits grabbed Philip for a boozy afternoon, and Jeff snuck off with Elsa in the middle of the house tour. Tanya quickly glommed onto Kamal and Ayeleen. Kamal looked at his sister desperately, so she grabbed me. I had already made a plan with Henry, who promised me a trip to see a man about a carpet, so the five of us headed off to a well-known spot for Iskender kebab. This was a famous regional dish of thinly cut grilled lamb, tomato sauce, pita bread, melted sheep's butter, and yogurt. A light lunch in the blazing heat. I couldn't even get through it. I ordered an ayran and a large bottle of water and sucked on my Dunhills.

After lunch, we walked around the town, dodging the advances of various carpet men to the shop Henry knew. We brought Kamal and Ayeleen, thinking some Turkish friends might increase our street cred and lower the price. Tanya tagged along half-heartedly to a place called "Special Carpet." It was dubious.

A gentleman called Omer was bowing and waving us inside a long, narrow space, the air heavy with aromatic smoke. There we were received by Fatma, his wife, and Yasemin, his daughter, who looked about fifteen. Omer waved Yasemin away while Fatma made sure we were all seated comfortably on cushions against the tapestry-covered walls. Then she seemed to dissolve into the fragrant atmosphere laden with clove and carpet fiber.

We introduced ourselves, and Omer nodded at Henry, impressed that we had come with reinforcements. When I said my name, he smiled broadly and said, "Ah, Ali. You Turk, too?"

"No, I'm ah, not Turk."

"Your name, it means noble in Arab. You sure you not Turk?" He winked at me.

"No, ah."

"Syrian?"

"No...."

"Kurd?"

Suddenly, Fatma and Yasemin rematerialized with trays containing a tall, elegant tea pot and six small, intricately cut glasses. Great. Hot tea. I was gasping for a cigarette, but I was quite sure if I lit up in here, the entire place would ignite.

The pouring ritual was elaborate, and when we were all served, Fatma and Yasemin receded once again into the ether.

"Okay," Omer began, "we start with school on carpet. Turk carpet is the best in the world. Why? I tell you. First, double-knotted. Each piece of yarn is looped twice through the weft, making the carpet sturdier and more durable. Turk carpet can be made of silk, wool, or a wool-and-cotton blend. Colors are made from all natural. Also, silk rugs are made from butterfly cocoons, not silk worms like the Chinese carpet. Each one is handmade. Each one is special and different." As he spoke, a young man was unrolling carpets from every corner of the room and flinging them in front of us in a pile. It was as if Omer could read my mind, or better my face, to know what I was looking for in size, color, and material.

Suddenly, as if in slow motion, a rug was unfurled before me. It was peachy rose, gold, and moss green with flecks of muted blue. It was perfect! It looked about seven by nine feet, and I could already see it in my sad, single person's shoebox studio that I still wouldn't be able to afford without my Dad paying the rent. I had determined I could spend $550 on a carpet and still have enough to finance a little travel and a lot of cigarettes. It would be the first permanent thing I had ever owned, purchased with my own money.

"Stop!" I cried. "What is this carpet?"

"Ah. This is very special piece. Very old. Very special. This is silk carpet, Ali. Silk and wool. My dear you have exquisite taste."

"How much is it, Omer?"

"This carpet very old, very special and much money. But for friend of Henry's, nine hundred dollars. Special price. I wrap for you to take on plane, free shipping."

"Of course, that is a good price for such a carpet. But I am sorry. I cannot pay more than five hundred."

"Five hundred is not possible, my dear. It is silk and has deep rose and gold color. Most valuable and precious. I have much regard for your taste, but alas, I cannot sell for less than eight hundred."

"I understand, Omer. You cannot lose money. I don't want

to insult you. I will have to buy an inferior rug elsewhere because I cannot afford eight hundred."

I nodded to the group to get up and move for the street. Their mouths were wide open.

"Thank you so much for the tea and the lesson, Omer. Now that I know what beautiful carpets look like, it will be impossible to find another I love so much. Thank you again. I apologize if I wasted any of your time." I stood, gave him a shallow bow, and walked away without looking back, past my friends, and halfway up the block.

"Wait! Ali, I make deal for you. $575. You not tell anyone you beat up Omer this way. Okay? I wrap for you now."

I am not proud to say I was a little aroused. "Thank you, Omer. You just made a girl's day." So I would smoke fewer cigarettes. Nothing like a little retail therapy to cheer you up, and a deal no less! My dad would be proud.

Next we checked into our accommodation. The place was clean and cool enough to be considered an upgrade from the camp. I'll leave it at that. Aggie and I agreed to room together. She hadn't yet returned from the British Invasion of Selcuk, so I got first dibs on the twin bed closest to the AC. I showered in the common ladies' room in the hall. Clean at last, I lay down on my bed and looked up at the plaster ceiling, my eyes feeling heavy as they followed the hypnotic circles of the ceiling fan. I quickly slipped into a dream.

I was floating in the pool on a raft at my parents' weekend home in Quogue. My mother, played by Fatma of carpet store fame, was suddenly shouting something at me through a megaphone. Her words were muffled but I thought I heard my name. "Allai Achar, Allai Achar." Allahu Akbar.

The early evening call to prayer snapped me back to

consciousness. The speaker was right outside my window. Oy. I looked over and saw evidence that Aggie had come and gone without my notice. Looking at the time, I hurried to dress and make myself look presentable. I put on the only sundress I had packed for the summer and was considering which shoes struck the best balance between good fashion and good sense when I heard voices in the hall indicating it was time to go. I grabbed the pair of very on-trend gladiator sandals I had custom-made in Santorini while on vacation with my parents and headed to join the others in the street. When in Rome, so to speak. Ally, you are hilarious!

We assembled for our special lecture in the ancient 24,000-seat theater at six-thirty. The site closed at seven, and the crowds were already filtering out. Our group, which now included Andrik as well as Ayeleen, moved down the bleacher-style seating toward the "stage." My wardrobe malfunction was obvious immediately. The soles of my sandals were smooth leather. Not rubber. No traction. The white marble of Ephesus, smoothed by time and the elements, made evident my fashion "don't." I clung to the nearly useless rope railing and baby-stepped, falling behind the others who rolled their eyes in judgment. Whatever. Slow and steady wins the race.

When I eventually lost my footing and nearly my teeth, it was Kamal who grabbed me by the waist, laughing, and helped me the rest of the way. I noticed Tanya glaring in our direction.

"Nice shoes," he teased. "Are you battling a lion tonight or just common sense?"

"Ughh! I thought they were cute with the dress."

"They are," Ayeleen added. Thank you, Ayeleen.

When we were all seated, Gerta, with Armand close by, stepped on stage and started the lecture. The air had cooled considerably, and it was almost pleasant. The sky softened as the sun went down, and a slight breeze blew in from the coast. Some members of the other dig were present. I specifically noticed the Austrian blond called Elsa sitting and chatting intimately with Jeff. Dicky sat with Turbo and was noticeably quiet—and hopefully sober.

"Za zeater vas constructed in ze Hellenistic Period, in za third zentury BC during the reign of Lysimachos, but zen during ze Roman Period, it vas enlarged and formed its current style zat is zeen today and is the largest in zis region. Za Ephesus zeater vas used not only for conzerts and plays, but alzo for religiouz, political, and philozophical discussionz and for gladiator and animal fightz...."

The lecture was interesting, but I was spacing out, mesmerized by the view and the surrounding architectural elements in the dimming daylight.

Gerta wrapped up her spiel. It was after seven-thirty, and the site was empty. Additional members of the Ephesus crew appeared carrying buckets filled with ice, cold beer, and bottles of raki. There were trays of meze and pita and an assortment of nuts. Drinks were passed around, and the group mingled. I took more abuse for my shoes, and Jeff took the opportunity to chime in, recalling my close encounter with the rotting animal carcass to the new audience. Apparently, they were all well-seasoned field archeologists and had made their fair share of vomit-inducing discoveries.

The party got a little looser and louder. Some music was added, courtesy of the Austrians, which was the expected Euro techno crap, and some of the less self-conscious started to dance on the stage. Really. The Europeans completely lacked inhibition. All that was needed was a little Ecstasy, and we'd have a proper Ibiza-style rave. So much for a summer of introspection and intellectual curiosity.

I refused an invitation to join the bacchanal, blaming my unsuitable footwear, and instead sat to the side with Kamal and Ayeleen, enjoying my drink and the nibbles and admiring the theater against the backdrop of the setting sun. The sky was a magnificent explosion of pink and orange, and then a deep velvety blue as night set in. The columns on the theater stage fell into darkness. The black mouths of the stage entrances gaped eerily in the background. Elongated human shadows danced along the wall and seemed to be swallowed into the dark. I heard Dicky's voice above the music.

"Bloody hell, Gerta. It's just a dance." He was tugging at her arm.

"Pleaze, Richard. You are still drinking too much. Lower your voize and zit down." Other members of both crews moved toward them, and I thought it might turn into a West Side Story–like rumble, when a scream from the other side of the theater stopped both the Jets and the Sharks in their tracks. We were all silent and someone killed the music. I thought maybe they were just changing the score for this scene. It was hard to tell because the theater acoustics had the sound bouncing everywhere, but the cries seemed to come from somewhere in the shadowed bleachers.

"Hello?" Turbo called "Who is that? Are you okay?"

Elsa shouted, "Elp! Iz Jeff. Elp pleaze!"

We could see her scrambling in the dark from an elevated passage to the side of the bleachers. Turbo produced a headlamp from one of his many pockets, and we followed him single file toward the direction of Elsa's cries. When we caught up with her, we could see her hair was a dirt-filled mess and her shirt was on backwards. She was pointing to a stairway that led down the back side of the elevated seating and wiping her tear-stained face. We followed Turbo's lit gaze to the bottom, and there lay Jeff Hynes wailing in pain and naked as the day he was born.

"What happened?" Someone asked, as if the answer wasn't obvious.

"He zlipped," whimpered Elsa. "No good shooz." Another fashion victim. I bit my tongue to avoid laughing and caught Kamal's eye. He gave me a wink.

We all turned away from the shameful scene except Turbo, who threw Jeff his windbreaker and waited with him for help. He couldn't get up, and it was obvious that another broken leg, at the very least, was the reason. Someone called an ambulance, and someone else called the lawyers. Aggie stayed with Turbo, upon his request, to wait for reinforcements. There was nothing for the rest of us to do, so we left to find more food and drink.

Given the evening's turn, I wasn't in the mood. I sat alone with my thoughts and my Dunhills in the hotel's roof garden, raking over the day's drama, earlier dramas, and dramas created by yours truly.

What made people, smart people, adult people, still act so irresponsibly, so rashly, seemingly without consideration or consequence? Was it love, lust? Was it ego? Or was it a need to feel filled up with something that felt good for a bit to push down things that felt bad?

I thought about school. Philip wasn't the first friend I had treated carelessly. The stress and lack of sleep had me in a bad place. It took its toll on me mentally, and I was depressed.

Sometimes you can consume a person like a bag of Doritos when you're down and then be left feeling equally nauseous and guilty. I had distanced myself from my family because I viewed them as a distraction. Every time I showed up to some obligation or another and took my foot off the gas at school, I paid for it. Plus, there was the Melanie situation.

I had relied on her so much for so long for support. Now I was facing a tightrope blindfolded and with no net. Meanwhile, she was being consumed by medical school as well as the prick, not to mention her own self-imposed death by jogging. She needed me just as much as I needed her, and I couldn't be there. I had never felt so worthless and alone. I looked and felt like shit. So much so that once while making a dawn coffee dash at the end of an all-nighter, I was intercepted by a homeless man who asked me if I was okay. He said I didn't look okay. I wasn't.

But what was going on here with this group? Was archeologist/historian a similarly isolating cult? Did they have too much time on their hands? Or were they too just using each other as disinfectant for their personal wounds?

Once upon a time, I dreamed of a glamorous life where I could travel constantly, meet people from around the globe, and discuss art, books, history, and architecture, avoiding the vulgarity of real life and, God forbid, employment. I had been living that life, and at the ripe age of twenty-six, I was exhausted. Maybe I was less interesting than I thought. Or maybe I was growing up a little. I slept soundly that night, waking only briefly when the last call to prayer reached out to me in the night, reminding me how far I was from home.

Miraculously, I slept through the five a.m. call to prayer, but by seven, the white light was piercing the plantation-shuttered windows of my room. I heard stirring in the hall and figured it was time to get up. I was alone again. Did Aggie ever come back last night? And if not, where did she sleep? After getting cleaned up and dressed, I partially unfolded my beautiful new carpet. Given the flatness of the weave, I determined I could probably fit it into my large backpack if I left most of my clothes behind. No problem. Short of my death sandals, there was nothing with me I would need in New York. I ran my hand over the intricate pattern and felt the contrasting texture of the wool and silk threads. This rug was the first piece of the new life that was waiting for me. It was my future. I couldn't wait to roll it out completely.

Breakfast was awkward. Kamal and Ayeleen headed to their home after Jeff's accident. They took Philip with them and Tanya was glum not to have been asked as well. She sat alone with Kat, who was also in a mood because her romantic plot to snare Turbo was foiled by Jeff's accident. They scowled from a corner of the hotel's roof garden, where breakfast was served. Aggie was already seated and waved me over to her table with Pano and Henry, but she was rushing out as I arrived, so I joined the boys. She had to get Dicky cleaned up and sort out Jeff, who was taken to a hospital last night in Izmir. Simon drove Turbo back to Aphrodisias early this morning to collect his stuff and would then drive him to Izmir to get Jeff on the plane. Aggie would be glued to a phone most of the day making sure his arrangements were in order, his parents were in the loop on his schedule, and everyone felt very taken care of and not like suing. So Jeff was headed stateside zero for two. Now I don't wish misfortune on anybody, but really. The guy enjoyed the misery of others a little too much. And karma is, as they say, a bitch.

Henry told me they had been discussing an idea for the five-day break mid-season. He, Simon, and Aggie planned to rent a car and drive to several sites up the west coast, including Bergama, Ayvalik, and maybe jump on a short ferry to Lesbos, Greece. Yes, Lesbos, the birthplace of Sappho, the famous ancient Greek poet and original lesbian. Henry also mentioned there was another place nearby worth visiting called Assos. I wanted to ask why that place was famous, but I was already giggling. They already had two boys and were shopping for another girl to bunk with Aggie. While they assumed correctly that I was useless and could not drive a stick shift, I was apparently the least of all the female evils. How could I pass on such an invite? Anyway, these three were the least controversial players in this drama. I had no other plans, so I accepted.

We had that day off, and the group planned to hit the beach. We would spend the day there, enjoy a seaside lunch, and drive back to the site in the late afternoon. The nearest beach, Pamukkale, was a fifteen-minute drive from Selcuk. Those of us still standing packed into the remaining van with all of our stuff after check-out. No one had yet dared to mention Jeff. But then Kat broke the ice.

"I can't decide whether I am more upset that Jeff got hurt or that the row between Gerta and Dicky was interrupted. It would have been very entertaining."

"You are all heart, Kat," Henry responded. "What have you got against Dicky?"

"Aside from the fact that he is a drunken imbecile? His carelessness and lack of focus have thwarted my every effort in the last fourteen months to defend my dissertation. I want to move on. I want to be in New York." Tanya was looking at her with raised eyebrows. "And now he has Aggie managing his bullocks and enabling him to appear marginally functional.

Nobody at Oxford will touch him. Aside from that, I don't fancy Jeff much either. I reckon I might have pushed him down the stairs myself if I'd had the chance. Skirt-chasing Neanderthal."

"Kat! That is so nasty! How can you say that?" Tanya asked.

"Really, Tanya? It's okay then to badmouth people one-on-one? Just not in a group? Right. Noted." We rode the rest of the way in silence.

When we arrived at the beach, I was pleasantly surprised. To be clear, it was no Hamptons with its crashing surf and wide grass-covered dunes, but the water was clean and very warm. A good bit of sea crap littered the line where the water broke. The shore was so flat you could step over the muck and walk a good way out to cool off and still be standing. We had neither lounges nor umbrellas, so we spread our towels right on the sand near the water's edge and got settled. Good thing I had my dad's coloring, or I swear I could have spontaneously combusted in the sun. I skeptically eyed the remaining Brits applying sunscreen.

Kat's comments put us all in a weird mood. Tanya was noticeably less chummy with her that day and stuck to Henry like glue. Kat kept her headphones on and buried herself in a book.

Pano and I took drink orders and walked to a café that was right on the beach. I was glad to have a minute with him. I wanted to ask him something I was embarrassed to verbalize in front of the others.

"Pano, can I ask you what might be an indelicate question?"

"I guess that would depend on how indelicate," he laughed and looked at me. "Sure, Ally. Go ahead."

"I know there are tensions between the Turks and Greeks," I started carefully. "I am sorry, but what is the history there?"

"Well, you know after World War I the Ottoman Empire was on the losing end and was broken up, yes?" I did know that. "So, at this time, a forced population exchange was made between Turkey and Greece. Muslims in Greece were forced to leave, even if they spoke Greek and their families had lived there for hundreds of years, and vice versa in Turkey. It involved millions of people and was devastating to those on both sides who were forcibly expelled from the lands their families may have occupied for generations, even centuries. Many were forced to travel by foot over long distances. Some were too young or old to make the journey and died along the way. Those who made it suffered discrimination and had a difficult time assimilating. That is the long and short of it, and the wounds are still raw today."

"Got it" was all I could muster in response. It was funny; I was raised to believe that Jews were always the targets, particularly in Europe. It never occurred to me that other ethnic groups experienced collective trauma and that their PTSD could similarly last generations.

I stared into the refrigerated cases filled with meze, or appetizers, while a young man filled our drink order. Lunch was looking very promising, and I could swear I caught a passing whiff of a pastry dessert tray oozing sweet buttered honey and nuts. We collected the drinks and headed back toward the group.

The rest of the day was uneventful. There was a dock about a hundred yards off the shore, and a group of us swam out to sunbathe there. I felt my batteries recharge in the warm, refreshing water. I forgot about Jeff and the bad luck that had him heading home without really getting started for the second year running. I forgot about the tensions and intrigues that plagued my site crew. I was without cares for the moment. A therapeutic day of swimming and eating in peace at a seaside café was my universe for the moment, and it was good.

We made it back to camp in time for dinner, which was quiet and more than a bit tense. Sober would be the word. There would be questions for the top brass to answer. Maybe consequences for less-than-responsible behavior. Grown-up stuff. Debbie still wasn't back, so there was a chance I could have some time alone. I kept my head down, grabbed a quick shower, and headed to bed to write Mel a letter. I was giving her the play-by-play via the post as best I could. I was eager to get her take on all of it.

CHAPTER 7

THE DAILY GRIND

After the departure of Jeff Hynes, life on the dig quickly got back to "normal." Various members of the dig rotated in on our survey group when they had time to fill his shoes. The heat continued to be oppressive, the bathroom situation abysmal, and showers only marginally effective. I had taken to stopping in the kitchen on my way to the shower house and shamefully using my toweled sexuality to inquire coquettishly "baklava var mı?" The first week I got shaking heads and downcast eyes responding, "Baklava yok." I responded to this by pouting and wordlessly retreating. Then one day I got smiles and nods and "Baklava var!" to which I responded with cheers and "Çok teşekkür ederim!" We had baklava every other day going forward. Almost never my ass.

Debbie's mood was particularly chirpy these days. I gathered her time alone with Andrik was responsible. She had taken to questioning me regarding Nina, his ex. In truth, I knew next to nothing about her. But that seemed to annoy Deb, so I asked what Andrik had told her and just added a little improvised color to his stories or comments. That cheered her up a bit. She was getting a letter from him almost every day, and that had her on cloud nine. She was still focused on her own research, but she was also working on Turbo's project to develop the city plan. She had her own digging crew as well as a fair number of Turks at her command. She was about my size, small, and not particularly outspoken. But when she stood on a wall or in a pit with her notebook, aviators, and Lawrence of Arabia headdress, she was a BOSS! When the surveying portion of my job was completed, I would be working with her documenting her excavation, and I was looking forward to it.

The week after Jeff's departure, I got a letter from Mel. She was all aflutter about her move to DC and especially her new car. She leased herself a little BMW to make the commute. It was the first car of her own, and she was feeling proud seeing her hard work and ambition bear fruit. I was happy for her, of course, and a little bit jealous if I was honest with myself. Mel had so much drive in school. She did not come to Penn with the same advantages as many of the kids in our circle, myself included. She did not wear this on her sleeve. She held down work-study jobs plus babysitting side-gigs for the scientist she interned with for extra cash. She did this on top of excelling in her premed classes, participating in our sorority, and always being down for whatever. And of course, managing to always be there for me with my self-indulgent complaints. We both had mommy issues and little sister issues, but Mel seemed better equipped to face them down. Or maybe it was more like to plow right through. It was one of the qualities I most admired about her, and now while I was still wallowing in self-pity and doubt, she was moving on. She would always be my best friend, but we were moving further from college every day, and there was no going back. I envied her.

She was very interested in the Debbie/Andrik, Turbo/Kat,

and Kamal/Tanya sagas. My mission was to continue to observe and report. As far as Philip was concerned, she didn't understand why I just didn't hop back in bed with him for sport. She thought his ego would allow him to go for another turn, hoping for a better outcome, and what the hell else was there to do here? I saw her point but couldn't do it for several reasons, the least of them being it might just be too hot to fool around here.

By the end of the third week, Simon, Henry, Aggie, and I were solidifying our plans for the upcoming break. We would travel steerage to Selcuk on Friday after work and spend the night. Saturday we would pick up the car and set off north. We would hit Pemukkale and then Bergama, the ancient city of Pergamon. This was another "upscale" ancient site. Our final stop was a couple of days in Ayvalik, the piss water 'Amptoms of my dreams! Given its location to the south, there would not be enough time to hit Bodrum and the legendary discotheque. I was not disappointed. I was bummed about missing Cappadocia, a region in central Turkey known for its underground cities. There was so much more of Turkey I wanted to explore. If I knew then what I know now, I would have bailed on those two weddings late in August in NYC and spent a month traveling.

Debbie was planning on spending her days with Andrik hopping from one Greek island to the next. How very romantic. Kamal was going home to be fed by his mother. Pano, Tanya, Kat, and Philip were headed south to Bodrum to club hop for a week. Good luck. I had seen Philip dance at school. The inflatables at a used car lot had better moves.

Until then, there was work to be done. Rise with the sun, hit the rocks, lunch, rest, more rocks, tea, jog, cocktails, dinner, sweat my ass off all night. Debbie and I were working together during the day. She was supervising the dig team as they uncovered a corner of the North Agora.

An agora was an open space in an ancient Greek city that served as a center of social, commercial, and political meetings. I followed the crew drawing every stone of the walls as they were found to scale on my pad of graph paper. It was quiet work, meditative, and very low stress compared to the pressure of school. I listened to music all day on my crappy yellow Walkman, which I'd had since junior high. I had only brought five tapes, which included three-quarters of a Bob Marley box set that covered his entire career from early days to greatest hits, Paul Simon's Graceland, and a Digable Planets' Reachin'. Random. With the first four, I made a schedule. Since each tape was about an hour, I would get through them twice each day. I did not need to look at a watch to know the time. I could gauge based on the music. The Digable Planets I saved for my runs. There is a line from the first track, "When we hit New York, Shazam!" that had been my rallying cry for the last three years. Frequently, tour groups would congregate around my ditch, and I would turn down my music and listen to the guide if they were speaking English. The guides would always wave to me and say hello like they were here every day and knew me. Then I would hear them explain where they were and what we were doing. Nearly one hundred percent of the time, they were bullshitting.

While I was still donning the cut-offs and tanks and cultivating what could only be described as a savage tan, I changed up my headgear to better conform. Besides, my huge hat was not only cumbersome but a challenge with old-school headphones. Debbie showed me how to soak a pillowcase in water and tie it to your head to keep cool and lock in the headphones. You had to carry an extra bottle of water to the field to re-soak mid-session, but it definitely helped. The outfit plus the head schmattah and the Jackie-O shades was a look I would be happy to retire in August.

I worked and kept my head down in the days leading up to the break until I had a conversation that would threaten to pull at the thin thread holding the group together.

I continued to spit in the face of the feminists that came before me by using my sexuality to get dessert. Any port in a storm. Headed for the showers, I saw the hose perv's sidekick eying me sheepishly from the back door of the kitchen and pretending to sweep. I took my hair out of the filthy scrunchie, adjusted my towel, and headed his way with a special spring in my step. As my father always told me, never show up to negotiate without the proper leverage.

"Alo," With a nod and a smile, I said, "baklava var mı?"

"Baklava var," answered Hose Perv from behind the door. The sidekick scampered away, and we were left face to face. I felt once again that my need for instant gratification had gotten the better of me, and now, I would pay. I feared this creep would attempt to exchange what was left of my virtue for dessert, and then I heard, "Your name is Ali, yes?"

"What? Uhh, yes, Ally."

"Deniz. I am Deniz." He was smiling and nodding his head. I was hiking up my towel. "You are mimar, uh, arkitec? Sorry. My English no so good."

"Better than my Turkish." I was speaking very loudly, laughing maniacally, and trying to back out of the kitchen. His brow furrowed. Maybe he didn't get it? He reached out and called, "Wait!" and I thought he was going to rip off my towel. I stumbled a bit in reverse and tried to yell, but nothing came out.

"Wait. Ali. I sorry. I try to speak to you because you first arkitec to speak to us. You come to say hello."

"Oh, well, uh." Oy.

"I have sister, Akara. She like, uhh, mimari. Buildings. She have nobody to talk to about. She want to learn. You talk to her?" He wanted a tutor for his sister, not to jump my bones. I was embarrassed and more than a little insulted, if I am being honest. Yes, I'm a sicko. I know.

"Why don't you ask Kamal? You know, the Turkish architect?"

"Akara cannot go with Kamal."

"But he knows so much about the dig, and he speaks Turkish."

"Akara cannot go with Kamal." He spoke deliberately and looked me right in the eye.

"Ah. Right. Well, what if the two of us met her? Kamal could help if she has trouble understanding." He considered this for a moment.

"Maybe out there." He pointed in the direction of the monuments. "Nobody can know. Big trouble for Akara."

"Yeah. Okay. Let me ask Kamal. Maybe during or after tea? I'll let you know. Deniz, I have to go now." I pointed to the shower house. He smiled and nodded.

"Okay, Ali. Thank you." He bowed a little and stepped away, and I took off for the shower house. Debbie was walking out.

"You just got here? What's that about?"

"Oh, nothing. I had to go back and get my razor. And yes, there is baklava tonight."

"Nicely done," she added, looking me up and down approvingly.

Later at cocktails, I tried to get Kamal alone for a second to ask him about helping Akara. He was kind of cornered by Tanya, and his eyes were shifting around, looking for rescue. He caught me looking his way.

"Hey, Ally! We missed you on our run today." I swear Tanya's eyes rolled. Bitch. "Sorry. I had some things I wanted to do."

I heard Philip scoff. "I'm sure. I saw you by the kitchens talking with the waiter. In your towel. Are we having baklava, Ali?" I really resented his tone, but I did not want to get into it in front of all of these people. The silence was deafening as we all sat there looking at each other. Thankfully, Deniz saved me by sounding the call for dinner.

I was really looking forward to a few days off. I would use the time to consider how to involve Kamal in my plan to help Deniz's sister.

CHAPTER 8

A TEMPORARY PARDON

Our road trip finally arrived. I stood in the road with Henry, Aggie, and Simon and waited for our ride to Selcuk. We opted to shower up quickly after work and immediately leave so that we would arrive at a decent hour and be able to enjoy dinner out to kick off the trip. The ride there was uneventful. Of course, there was the usual baptism by lemon-scented liquid, a single bored goat, and then a quiet ride. I blew smoke mindlessly out an open window in the back.

We checked into our usual cheap, air-conditioned hotel and hit the streets for dinner. I was looking forward to some seafood. The food on the dig was OK, all things considered, but I was sick of eggplant boats, kofta, and the thought of that goat shank still made me gag. We were subjected to the usual cat calls from carpet vendors as we window-shopped the menus and eventually settled on a place. It was a pleasant night, not too hot, and this was low-drama company. I listened to Simon talk about his little boy and Aggie discuss the progress of Turbo's book with Henry. I sipped wine and smoked cigarettes and spaced out a bit, enjoying the reprieve from the soap opera–like site.

The next morning, we picked up the car and headed out

early toward Pamukkale, which literally means "cotton castle." It is a natural site about three hours from Selcuk, famous for carbonate-rich mineral springs and thermal pools. Spas. Yes, please. You could get a decent hotel with a pool and AC plus an en-suite bathroom for twenty-five to thirty dollars per night. Ours was a half mile from the Cleopatra Pools, which were mineral springs and a pool where you could swim amongst Roman ruins.

Nearby, there was a breathtaking landscape of snow-white travertine created by epochs of mineral deposits pocked by thermal pools. All of this sounded very promising. I grabbed some brochures the night before in town and was studying them in the car to the tune of the only English-language radio station we could find blaring out bad eighties pop music and worse disco. I noticed someone else had added a pamphlet on Hierapolis, another ancient Roman city. Shit.

Generally, I was a big fan of what my parents called "hot rocks," but between Aphrodisias,

Ephesus, and the prospect of Bergama/Pergamon, I was good for a while. A little less schlepping in the heat and a little more relaxing in natural springs was in order, and no less part of the "Turkish experience," I might add. Pamukkale is a UNESCO World Heritage Site. Sitting in a mineral bath was no less legitimate sightseeing than Hierapolis. Still, I needed to make sure we were all on the same page.

"So, guys, what is the plan for Pamukkale?"

Aggie was first, "Well, we cannot check in until four p.m., but the hotel said we can still hang out and use the pool until then." Well said, Aggie. Couldn't agree more.

"Well, it won't quite be lunch by the time we get there. Why don't we hit the Cleopatra Pools then find some lunch? Then if there is time, we could hit the spring. That way we could take it easy tomorrow before setting off for Bergama." Thank you, Henry. Excellent point, better plan.

"Isa loong day, init? Recon weed'ave time fa Hierapolis if we're to get an early enuf stat tumorra? Wee cud grab sandwiches fa the ca hit tha springs and pool taday? Thin tha nearby ain't they?" I wasn't certain, but it sounded like Simon was the weak link. He was front loading my relaxing vacay. I caught Aggie's eye in the rear view.

"I'm sorry, Simon. We weren't planning on hitting Hierapolis this time. Henry and I have both been there a few times, and Ally, well, we figured she might be more keen to rest up tomorrow morning before Pergamon after such a long day today."

"Right ch'are. Bin thar me self. If ya shur ya don mine, Ollie? Wuddin wanna cheatcha!" He laughed. I laughed too, nervously, because I still wasn't sure where we stood. Henry saved me.

"Thoughtful of you, Simon. Thanks. She's good. We already convinced her," and he winked at me. "We can do pools, lunch, and springs today and take our time tomorrow and just do Pergamon. That's enough for one day for sure!" Relieved, I smiled at Simon and got back to my pamphlets.

We rolled up to the dirt parking lot of our hotel around eleven. I jumped out of the car and darted through the small lobby, repeating "Tuvalet nerede?" to anyone who looked at me. Over the years, my tiny bladder has been the impetus in my learning to ask "Where is the toilet?" in almost twenty languages.

I took my time walking back to the car to collect my bag, surveying the place. It looked clean. I could see the neat pool to the rear and white mounds of carbonate "beach" beyond.

Beach with no sea. Henry had already made them aware of our arrival, and we were instructed to return closer to four p.m. to check in. We would walk the half mile to the Cleopatra Pools and scout out a fine spot for lunch on the way. We could enjoy a long, late lunch on the way back and spend the rest of the day at the mineral springs. It was Sunday, so the place was clearing out. We packed day bags with towels and dry clothes and headed out.

The walk to the Cleopatra Pools was just ten minutes. One full cigarette. Back then, a smoke for me was not only an instant Xanax but also an appetite suppressant, conversational tool to add a pregnant pause, and a way to fill time in ten-minute intervals. I knew how bad it was for me, but really couldn't give it up. The fear of a painful, preventable future death for an otherwise healthy twenty-something woman times the price of cigarettes is less than the sum of her vanity plus her anxiety times her physical addiction. There is an actual equation to prove this.

There wasn't much of a town in between the hotel and the pools. We did pass some promising cafés. The menu was generally the same at every restaurant in this part of Turkey, so for me it was mostly about the "ambiance." Weird smell? No thanks. Tables faced a well-trafficked street? I'll pass.

Finally, there was a spot with "garden seating" shaded by a mature apricot grove on three sides and a view of the mineral plains to the north. We were on the tail end of the apricot season in Turkey, but there were still a few on the lower branches, and the place was lovely. I nodded my approval to the rest of the group and lit up again in celebration. On to the pools.

Apparently Cleopatra herself did not only swim in these

warm, clear water pools, which once included a Roman Temple to Apollo, with an ornate roof, Doric columns, and all, she preferred them to the milky white waters of the mineral plain. It was pretty magical, save for the presence of other tourists. Luckily, by the time we got there and got settled, it was almost lunchtime, and the tourist groups were thinning out.

I saw some people filling water bottles from a hand-operated pump and drinking. I had an empty bottle in my pack. I considered the risk. I remembered my childhood trips to Mexico and how my physician grandfather always prescribed a two-week course of Greek yogurt in advance to put the right bacteria in your gut and stave off Montezuma's Revenge. He was ahead of his time regarding probiotics. I had eaten enough real yogurt over the last month to safely drink from the Ganges. I was still weighing the odds when a zaftig older lady in a smaller bikini than mine and a lit cigarette with two in ash marched up to me, saying, "Go! Girlie! Go! Take vater to keep your beauty! Drink to stay young," and she gave my face a little slap. Russian. I was stunned and stood stock-still, frozen like a statue. Aggie grabbed me, shaking with laughter.

"Ally, you can drink the water. It is safe. Legend says it has health and beauty benefits. And obviously, there is danger in *not* drinking it." Her body was still shaking a bit from stifled giggles when it was my turn at the pump. I filled my bottle and moved on.

Like the great Queen herself, I waded into the warm waters and explored the fallen columns and other artifacts sitting in the stillness below. I found a solitary, quiet corner and shut my eyes, blocking out the noise. I was recalling my last former–Soviet slap down during a spa trip to Margaret Island, Budapest, in my college days, when Aggie sidled up, still giggling to herself over my assault.

"Sorry, Ally. You should have seen your face."

"Believe it or not, it was not the first time I took a slap from a Russian."

"I would not doubt it," she said, raising an eyebrow.

We surveyed the scene. It was pretty cool to see the ruins below the surface. I was surprised they weren't more covered in algae or other yuck. I guess the minerals kept that at bay. The bubbles were remarkable! The mineral pool was effervescent, which felt great. It was like swimming in San Pellegrino. P and H would love this. They were great travelers but had completely dismissed Turkey as a civilized destination. They were definitely paranoid about being Jews traveling in a Muslim country. Additionally, the lack of premium fashion brands for my dad to scoop up, discounted due to the exchange, added to my mother's inability to speak Turkish, rendered Turkey a non-starter. Phyllis was a retired language teacher and spoke five languages. She was judgmental in all five.

We moved through the water to a less crowded area surrounded by lush planting. There was a plaque to the side showing a reconstruction of the ancient site with the temple intact. I tried to imagine what it might have been like almost two thousand years ago to enjoy these pools, in near privacy and silence.

The afternoon crowds were growing again as tour buses continued to pull up and regurgitate foreign tourists at the gate. Around me, Russians were posing for bikini shots, Germans were stripping off damp bathing suits without an ounce of modesty, and the only English to be heard came from the mouths of lobster-red Brits. This place may have been somewhat spoiled, but not yet by Americans for a change. It was time to go. I could see my colleagues were on the same page. Henry was lending Aggie a hand getting out, and Simon was already headed for the men's locker room. I hustled to catch up with them and almost ran straight into my corpulent assailant, who stood bent with her back to me, drying her ample legs. I switched directions to avoid being further accosted.

Once we were all dried and dressed, we headed out for lunch. I had my wet bathing suit knotted to the outside of my bag so it would dry before our afternoon trip to the travertine pools. We found the garden café we had scoped out earlier. It was already after one-thirty p.m. by the time we sat down, and I was more than ready for lunch. The best thing to eat at all of these places was the mezze, or small appetizer plates. You could sample many different things without committing to one dish. I was pretty easygoing when it came to ordering. As long as we could avoid gross animal parts and deep-fried everything, I was happy to let a more seasoned traveler of Turkey do the honors for us all. I ordered a glass of wine and excused myself to use the bathroom, planning to smoke a quick cigarette on the way back.

I found a cool spot hidden in the apricot grove to finish. Nobody in Turkey cared what or where you smoked, but I just wasn't ready to join the group. There were buckets burning citronella, and the flames burned dangerously close to the fruit-laden low branches that moved lazily in the pleasant breeze. Aggie joined me and bummed a smoke. Funny, I had never noticed her smoke at the dig. In truth, there was so much drama, I barely noticed her at all. I looked at her closely now through my dark shades as we quietly pulled on our smokes. She was a little shorter than I was. Her shoulder-length blond hair sat in curls around her face and bounced when she talked and laughed, which she did a lot. She was quiet and sweet and seemed completely without ulterior motives or personal agenda, which made her different from most of the others.

"You okay, Ally?" she asked when she noticed me staring.

"Sure. Thanks. I'm just... enjoying the break, from work and the heat." We both laughed a little.

"It's just I imagine you must feel out of sorts here sometimes, not being a regular. I mean you're not an archeologist or historian. I'm sorry I don't mean to.... You just seem somewhere else sometimes. Or that you'd rather be."

"No. You are right. I am for sure a one-timer. I'm not insulted. I am out of sorts sometimes, but really overall I am enjoying it. It's an incredible opportunity. Once in a lifetime. If I seem only half in sometimes, I'm just thinking."

"About?" Okay. She was nosier than I thought. I didn't want to say too much. I had learned not to trust people with my private thoughts, and this group was so mercurial.

"My family. My sister in particular. She just had a baby." I smiled thinking about my cutie niece. My sister sent me some photos of her on the beach in East Hampton sleeping in a little screened-in baby pod. "I sometimes feel like I'm missing something."

"Forgive me, but why? Your niece will still be there when you get back. She'll still be a baby in fact. You are not her mother. What do you feel you are missing? You said yourself: you are a 'one-timer' here. So, enjoy it. Or at least, let the rest of your life wait a few more weeks."

She was right. She wasn't my child. How much could I really see her or help now anyway? They were out east most of the time. I would just be pounding the pavement in town, looking for a job and an apartment and eventually working all week. I could make up a few lost weekend hours when I got home for sure.

"Ah, the food!" She stamped out her cigarette and headed back to the guys. The detachment of the English was just what I needed to break the spell of Jewish guilt. At least for the moment.

The table was covered with small plates including grilled squid, lamb sausages, grilled veggies, some kind of fried cheese, dips, and, of course, pita. The meal and the wine resolved my hunger as well as some of my lingering reservations. For the first time since my arrival in Turkey, I felt the sense of peace and enthusiasm that usually accompanied my adventures.

We took our time at lunch. We knocked off a couple of bottles of wine and the better part of a pack of my smokes. By the time we finished our coffee, it was almost three p.m. Feeling rested and relaxed, and a bit buzzed, we headed for the springs, changing back into our now-dry suits in the restaurant's WC. The walk was a leisurely twenty minutes and woke us all up. We reached the travertine terraces just before three-thirty. By then, the dense crowds had pretty much cleared out, and you could find a corner where you could look out and see nobody, nothing but the dazzling white petrified lime cascades. We stripped down to our suits and waded in. The view was breathtaking, although I was afraid I would find the water too hot in the heat of the afternoon. The coolest of the waters was close to a hundred degrees. Some springs were boiling!

Obviously, we avoided those. I was pleasantly surprised to find the water quite soothing. The high mineral content had me floating around the top, like the Dead Sea in Israel. Henry grabbed me laughing, and we bobbed like apples together over to the edge of the stone shelf. We held on, looking off into the distance in silence for a good while.

"So, are you glad you came?" he asked finally.

"On this trip? Definitely. I really had no idea Turkey was so amazing. If I am honest, it was not on my radar. I wish I had more time to travel at the end. There are still so many places I want to visit."

"No, I mean on the dig. Sometimes it seems, well, like you're not so into it."

"So I hear. Look, I'm not going to lie. It might be a little more rustic than I anticipated. I don't know what I expected.... I'll be honest. I think the people were more of a surprise."

"What do you mean?" He was laughing.

"Well, I don't know how to say this so that it doesn't sound bitchy. I mean, I think everyone is nice and really bright and accomplished in their field of focus..."

"But..."

"But I guess I thought people would be, well, better behaved. In general. Sometimes I feel like I'm tiptoeing through a minefield."

He sighed. "Yeah, well, it's a long haul, a PhD. And after all the time and money spent, you are lucky if you get a position at a great university, or even a decent one in a real place. Most don't. You could end up teaching antiquities in Kansas." I feigned (only partially) horror.

He went on. "And even if you get that position, you are not guaranteed tenure. Guys like Turbo are the luckiest. Tenured position in a first-rate NYC university? It's like the fuckin' holy grail... and there is still no money in it. Even if you are regularly published."

I laughed. "So, I guess you all feel entitled to live like a horde of adolescents?"

"Well, I wouldn't say that... but I guess it is fair to say all of that uncertainty and delayed gratification makes some a little, well, careless."

"I get it. I have felt that way myself at times."

"So I hear." He raised his eyebrows, and I looked away into the distance.

"If you mean Philip, I am done apologizing for that. He was a good friend and then for a minute he was more, and it wasn't right so now he is not even my friend. Anyway, it was a while ago. He needs to let it go." I had never heard myself be so straightforward, but that was how I felt. I wanted to be a grown-up and move forward, even if he preferred to play up the drama with these people, I was done trying to explain myself... about this at least. Nobody was hating on Andrik for dumping Nina, forget about moving on so soon. And they were a serious couple. Why was there a double standard?

"That is what I told him. Anyway, it is none of my business. Sorry. I just think he really liked you."

I nodded, saying nothing. What could I say? That liking me right now was like jumping overboard with a bucket of concrete? I had come here to lick my wounds and lay low for a while. That was true. But I also wanted to come home armed to face my future. I wasn't going to find anything in this crew to fortify me. But maybe looking outward for strength and validation wasn't the key. Maybe I had to stop seeking strength and approval in others altogether.

"Ally? Are you okay?"

"Yeah. I am, Henry. I'm fine," I muttered unconvincingly, even to myself.

We found the others. Aggie, who was the most knowledgeable, spoke a little about the site and its history and conservation. I was only half listening, looking off into the distance at the landscape. I imagined how vast the world of the Greeks and Romans must have seemed compared to the world we know now. I thought about how even less than a century ago travel such as I had experienced was nearly impossible for most in a lifetime, never mind in less than a decade. And for a woman?

What would be next? It was 1998. I was a bit of a Luddite, even at twenty-six. I was dreading the prospect of learning computer drafting. I would have to if I wanted a job. Many of the people I had finished school with had already embraced it. And what about this "email" and "downloading music"? I would have to learn to walk toward the things that scared me instead of running away.

It was almost five p.m. when we finally made it out of the pools. We dried ourselves and dressed over our wet suits in the parking lot. The hot soak in the heat made me a little light-headed, and a long drag of my cigarette almost knocked me over. I walked to a souvenir truck for water and saw my Russian sparring partner. She stood unapologetically in her barely existent bikini, eating an ice cream from a case. She pinched her own cheek and gave me a thumbs up.

By the time we returned to our pension, the rooms were ready. We agreed to shower and meet in the garden for cocktails at six forty-five. We would then move onto another pleasant meal at a place we had scoped out on our way back from the pools.

The rooms were fine. Clean and basic. And they had air conditioning. Heaven. The bathroom had a tiny stall shower and questionable toilet plumbing, but it was ours alone, and I was grateful. I showered early and lay down to read for a bit before getting dressed.

Maybe it was the heat or the pools, but I suddenly felt the weight of my body and drifted off to sleep almost as soon as my wet head hit the pillow. I dreamed I was having tea. I was sitting in a Turkish carpet shop on a pile of cushions in front of a low table. There were five glass tea cups and a plate of almond cookies. My parents were there, and my sister. But there were five cups. Who were we missing? They all poured themselves a cup and started nibbling cookies and chatting away about my niece, my sister's eventual return to work, etc. But who were we still missing? How come nobody offered me any tea? Or a cookie? A sense of anxiety filled me, and I felt myself sinking into the cushions. Nobody noticed, and I was sinking, sinking, until I was almost drowning in the thick, deep upholstery. I cried out, but it was not my voice yelling "Allah!"

Call to prayer. I was awake, and Aggie was staring at me toweling off her hair. "Alright then, are we?"

"Yeah, just a weird dream. What time is it?"

"Gone six. You might want to get up."

"Shit." I jumped out of bed and scrambled to put myself together. My restless slumber left me a little sweaty. Or maybe that was my damp head? Anyway, I rinsed my face and slicked back my mad hair. Ten minutes later, I was ready to go, sporting my sundress and the infamous gladiator sandals. Low risk tonight. Flat streets of mostly packed dirt. A swipe of lip gloss, and I was standing by the door waiting for Aggie, the small woven pouch I had purchased in Selcuk dangling from its strap on my wrist. She turned to me, shaking her head.

"I don't know how you manage it."

"What?" I had no clue what she meant.

"Nothing! Or at least very little. And there you are. Always so put together. To look at you, I'd say you were high maintenance. But really, it is effortless."

That was probably the nicest thing anyone had ever said to me. Or at least the thing I most appreciated.

"Thank you, Aggie. Please know, I still generally feel half-wrecked most of the time."

"Well, I can't believe that." She grabbed her clumsy, oversized purse and walked past me to the hall. Okay. To her point, I could always work an accessory. But still, her words made me feel like a million bucks. Why couldn't I have the kind of confidence that compliment suggested I had?

We joined the others in the torch-lit garden just before six-thirty. The sun was starting to retreat and with it the heat. We sipped our drinks and nibbled pistachios. The dig felt a world away.

When we got to dinner, we decided on just ordering a ton of mezze. Simon seemed the most enthusiastic about it, so I nominated him to order for the table. We were all pretty easygoing; he was a seasoned Turkish traveler, and I frankly thought it would be amusing to see if he got further with his heavy Manchester accent than I could with my shit knowledge of the menu. Much to my surprise and delight, he did.

Within minutes, plates of garlic-laden dips, meat-filled veggies, and a grilled bounty from the sea arrived with the customary boat of yogurt, more garlic, and a pile of piping hot pita.

"Awh, that's brilliant, innit?" he chirped as he scooped portions onto each of our plates with a gusto that would make you think he was the chef.

"Simon, you certainly seem to have a passion for Turkish food," I noted.

"Me mum is Turkish. From Cyprus. Came to Manchester

back when a Turks 'ad the troobles dar."

"Ah, wow," I answered like I understood what he said.

The meal was great. I had a belly full of Turkish food and wine and a cigarette pressed between my lips. The night was cool enough to generate a soft, refreshing breeze. We sat for a while talking. A little about US and UK politics. I just sat and listened, enjoying my own silence.

Later, back at our pension, washed and tucked into my clean bed in my coolish room, I sat and started a letter to Mel about the pools, the lime terraces, and the yummy dinner. I felt Aggie looking at me.

"You okay, Aggie?"

"Yeah, sure. Fine. You?"

"Fine. Tired. Long day. But dinner and the wine hit the spot."

"Yes, yeah." She paused. "Can I ask you something? It's a bit awkward."

I put down my letter and looked at her directly. "Sure, Aggie. What's on your mind?"

"Promise you won't repeat this? I just... I just don't feel I can talk to anybody else because, well, it's like—"

"I know." I interrupted. "Go ahead if you want to."

"Well. It's Rob Turbo." I already knew what she was going to say. "I am Dicky's assistant up at Oxford. And granted, he is a job. He can be rude and dismissive. And he is obviously a mess of a drunk. Really, sometimes I feel like his handler. But I know he appreciates me in his weird way and would be lost without me. And he is never inappropriate in that way." Her eyes widened. "But Turbo. Well, he is so.... And he is married. But even if he wasn't, no thank you. I just want to finish my work with Dicky and my degree. Turbo keeps saying he is trying to 'steal me' to come finish my research with him in New York. Like he would be doing me a favor getting me away from Dicky. How great it would be for us to work together. And to make it worse, I know... well I think Kat... well I think she fancies him. Maybe there was something more? I don't know..." She trailed off a bit. "Anyway, she's not been very kind to me. As if I want his attention. I don't know why I am telling you this. It's just been making me feel shitty since I arrived." I had never heard her curse. She seemed so proper it made me smile.

"Between you and me, Kat seems a little, well, high-strung. I wouldn't make too much of it. Wasn't she trying to get to New York this year anyway?"

"Yeah, but I don't think it's going to come off. Turbo has been treating her like a bad smell this year, and Dicky will never let her go. I think that is really why she's taking it out on me. Anyway, I just want Turbo to leave me alone. I am afraid his rejection of Kat will get her so angry she'll start rumors implying that I am, well, carrying on with him. You know. To benefit my prospects. That would ruin things for me in England for sure. And no offense, I have no desire to come to New York."

"I'm sorry, Aggie. Really. I know how you feel, well, not about New York," I joked, "but once you get back to Oxford, you'll have more space to avoid her and three thousand miles between you and Turbo."

"Thanks, Ally." She smiled. "Good night." She shut off her light and turned away. I worked a little longer on my letter and shut mine off as well. I could tell she was still awake, thinking, and I felt for her. Dealing with a bitch was easy enough. Little girl stuff. Sexual harassment, on the other hand, that was big girl territory indeed. At this stage in the game, I had no practical experience in that department. I had been on the receiving end of more than one inappropriate suggestion, but never with a quid pro quo attached.

We took our time the next morning. By the time Aggie and I met up with Simon and Henry for breakfast at nine, they were already seated at a shaded table with a view of the small pool and patio. Simon was reading an English paper. Aggie grabbed my arm when they waved us over.

"Ally, about what I said last night. I'm afraid all of that wine loosened my tongue. I really shouldn't have."

"Aggie, your concerns are legitimate. It is none of my business to discuss what you told me with anybody. But if you need someone to talk to, or even just vent, you can always come to me. I am not a player in this game, and I don't trade in other people's secrets."

She smiled and squeezed my hand. "Thank you."

We joined the guys and, as expected, Simon had already ordered breakfast. Fresh cheese, juicy, sweet apricots, and bread were on the table. Coffee was en route from the kitchen in a large silver pot with steamed milk, continental style. We lingered over breakfast and decided a couple of hours poolside would do us all some good. Then we planned to get started for Bergama before noon, grab a snack to go at a rest stop, and arrive at our hotel before four p.m.

The pool at our pension was not heated, but it was so hot by ten that the cool water was refreshing. I took a dip and then settled myself on a chaise under a pergola thick with the trained branches of a lemon grove. I sported my enormous beach umbrella hat and the five-dollar pair of Jackie O's I bought on the street near Howard's office. I could still hear him lecturing me about UV protection and polarized lenses. In my black maillot and tortoise-pattern jelly flip-flops, I did feel a little glamorous. I spied Aggie eyeing me from her spot in the sun next to Simon. What was with the British? Pasty white and eager to burn like lobsters the minute the sun came out. Must be all of that rain. Feeling like the Princess of Monaco, I sipped on iced apricot juice from a champagne flute and finished my letter to Mel, spilling all of Aggie's secrets. Aggie didn't say I couldn't tell anyone, just not the group. And anyway, Mel always had something sage to add. That is what best friends thousands of miles away were for.

The road trip to Bergama was uneventful. The somewhat green, broad Menderes River valley gave way to hillier terrain toward the ancient city once known as Pergamon We touched the outskirts of more urban areas as we neared Izmir, not too far from our destination. I noticed more of that odd construction with the rebar left on the roof like stubbly hair growth.

We were more than halfway there and making good time when we stopped at a roadside café to use the restrooms and grab a quick bite to go. I was a little hesitant to eat a street meat sandwich, so I grabbed a yogurt from the little shop. When we were back in the car, I regretted it immediately. The lamb smelled delicious and everyone survived. I sucked on a cigarette to drown out the savory olfactory assault.

We pulled up to our hotel just after four p.m. It was very quaint and clean and equipped with the all-important AC. It was an older stone structure with simply decorated "Turkish style" rooms. There was a charming garden and a rooftop view of the acropolis of ancient Pergamon itself. We had chosen it for its high Frommer's marks as well as its proximity to the little village. There were other hotels with pools, but really, we intended to do Pergamon hard the next day and power on to the

Ayvalik. So we opted for charming convenience for the night.

Dragging from the drive, we headed for our rooms to rest and get cleaned up. We planned to meet at the roof garden for drinks at six and be off to dinner by seven. The hotel room had an en-suite bathroom. I bolted for the first shower while Aggie settled in. With the somewhat hot water washing over me, I closed my eyes and thought again about what she told me the night before. I never gave sexual harassment any thought. I had been lucky enough to get through college, grad school, and a few stupid jobs and internships without any grab-assy bosses or lecherous professors. Maybe I wasn't as cute as I thought? Couldn't be. Guess I just had a sign on me that said, "Don't you fucking dare."

I had a few friends in college who claimed to be recipients of indecent proposals, but I never thought too much about it. It wasn't something we talked about in the nineties. That was something that happened on cheesy sitcoms, and those girls were the types that everything seemed to happen to anyway, right? This was my conditioning. That it was exaggerated or... encouraged somehow because it never happened to me. It had been seven years since Anita Hill testified before the Senate, and they confirmed Thomas anyway while the country moved on like it never happened. Meanwhile, my fellow women were currently being "me too'ed" all over the country, and Linda Tripp and Monica Lewinski were about to expose the president as the "Douchebag-in-Chief." It would be years still before women became more vocal about this and normalized exposing these guys. All that was certain to me at that moment was poor Aggie had Turbo breathing down her neck. She was a hard worker and a passionate historian. She didn't deserve to have her reputation, not to mention her future, jeopardized by this overaged adolescent who couldn't keep it in his pants. Regardless of what happened to her, he would go on unscathed and tenured at a top university. She could end up teaching history to secondary schoolers in Essex... or worse, Nebraska. It wasn't fair.

When I was done dressing, I grabbed my cigarettes and headed to the roof garden, borrowing some of Aggie's notes on Pergamon. I figured she was entitled to a little time to herself, but really, I wanted to read a little about the site in advance of our visit. I knew I was traveling with historians and specialists, but all I wanted to do was walk the acropolis alone until I found some shade and sit with a cigarette in my mouth, sketching. As a budding architect, that was totally acceptable.

There was a welcome breeze in the shade of the roof garden. From the corner of the olive grove, I could see the acropolis in the distance. An adolescent with a face like an icon and an apron around her waist was suddenly standing next to my table, smiling at me. I sputtered out something that sounded like coffee, to which she replied, "Simit?" I just smiled, and she scuttled behind a bar counter with a click of her tongue. I lit up and pondered the view. She returned with my tiny cup and something that looked like a sesame bagel. I pointed to it with raised eyebrows, to which she replied, "Simit!"

"Ah." Cig smoked, too-sweet coffee drained, and weird bagel noshed, I got to my studies.

Pergamon rose in importance and prestige throughout its long history of wars and alliances during the Hellenistic period. While the relationship with the Romans before the second century CE had its ups and downs, the reign of Trajan from 98–117 CE solidified Pergamon as a proper Roman metropolis, elevating it above its rival cities Ephesus and Smyrna. Trajan and his successors engaged in a massive program of redesign and remodeling, resulting in a new stadium, theater, temples, and a huge forum and amphitheater. The acropolis was built into the side of a mountain, resulting in one of the steepest theaters in the world. The views would be incredible. Of course, they built a kick-ass spa. Nobody did excess like the Romans! Then, in the middle of the third century, an earthquake knocked the city to its knees, followed shortly after by a good Goth sacking for the knockout punch. Typical. Feeling very much in the know regarding all things Pergamon, I tapped out my cigarette and waved over Simon and Henry. I looked at my watch and saw it was nearly six. I was ready for a drink.

"Studying up to school us all, Ally?" Henry winked.

"Dun thin ya can out sma me on Pergama. Thas how I met me wife. She wa assistan to me prof at Uni. Went to extra 'elp evy week I did until she agreed to 'ave a pint wid me."

"No, I just wanted a little background. If I am honest, I never heard of Pergamon, or most of these places, before coming here. I thought if I knew a little history, I could just walk the acropolis and get a better feel for the place."

"Where's Aggie?" Henry asked.

"I left her in peace to get ready. I hope she didn't fall asleep."

"Right. Do I hear my name in vain?" Aggie looked refreshed at the top of the stairs.

"Ya looky. We dying of furst and bout to get on wi'out ya." Simon waved over my aproned friend and ordered a bottle of white wine from Permukkale. He uttered some additional words I did not know and made some weird gestures with his fingers. The waitress nodded and disappeared. When she returned, she had the wine in an ice bucket and some small plates of seasoned olives, toasted pita, cheese, and nuts. Nailed it again, Simon.

The sky started to change colors as we sipped our drinks and nibbled our snacks. Between the booze and the freedom, we were all in a great mood. No pervy profs, book deadlines, or salty exes here. Some more people came and went. Simon kept ordering snacks and wine, and before we knew it, the sun was setting.

"Simon, I think we've missed our reservation, haven't we?" Aggie was looking at her watch.

"Dun mine. Da any of yoo? It's a'rite 'ere with the voo and the breeze an' all. Look!" Simon pointed to the acropolis. It was beautifully up lit and the sky was a cacophony of color around it. Truth be told, I was quite buzzed and pretty full. I was perfectly happy to stay put.

"Les rest 'ere and make an early nigh'."

We looked at each other and nodded in agreement. The sky was eventually a vast ink shroud glittering with stars. New York has so many great views, but if you want a stellar light show, you've got to get away from the city.

The early night got later and later, and eventually we were the only ones left on the roof. We settled into a handful of ancient chaises facing the acropolis. We were short one for Henry, so he put two upright chairs together and stretched out his legs. We sat quietly for a while, passing around my dwindling pack of cigarettes.

"Simon," I probed, "I don't think I ever asked. What is your little boy's name?"

A faraway smile filled his face. "Oliver. Severus Oliver really. He wus born 'bout twenty mina befa tha bleedin book came out. Now 'e 'as the name of a tossa wizard, 'e dos. We callin' 'im Oliver or 'es gonna have the shit knocked outta 'im fa sha." We were all laughing. "'Es walkin' now 'e is, the lit'le bugga. Me poor wife is tearin' 'er 'air out keepin' up. I missed it though. I missed it." He was a little choked up.

"I'm sorry, Simon. I know it is not the same thing, but I know a little of what you're feeling. My sister gave birth in May, and I skipped town a few weeks later. For the first time in my life, I feel like I am missing something. I always wanted to live abroad, like in Barcelona. Now, I just want to get back to NYC. Like my life is happening whether I'm in it or not."

"I would have thought nothing happens anywhere unless you are there, Ally," Aggie winked at me.

"So did I!" I said, laughing. "I underestimated how tough it really is for me to live untethered. How do you guys do it for so long? Not you, of course, Simon." Henry and Aggie looked at each other.

"Well," Henry exhaled deeply through his nose and ran a hand through his phantom head of hair, "I think it started with a desire to travel as an undergrad. Once you taste blood, you are hungry for the whole world. Antiquities just became the means. Then before you know it, you are on the other side of twenty-five, and people start to pair up. It becomes easier to be with and socialize with other nomads because they get it and don't have unreasonable expectations." Aggie was nodding in agreement.

"I get that," I chimed in. "I felt that way in grad school. I could barely talk to civilians."

"Yeah." He went on, "So before you know it, you are pushing thirty and have never had a 'real job' and belong to this kind of club of PhD smarties who know too much about shit nobody cares about, and you tell yourself it is for a higher purpose, but really you want to live like a student forever, travel free, and have a proper summer vacation. Part of me wants to chuck it and teach ancient history to middle schoolers. Still get the summer off. Just don't think I could deal with the little bastards."

We were all laughing. I wasn't the only one who hadn't figured shit out or was frankly running away from figuring shit out. We stayed up a little longer. Facing the breathtaking backdrop of Pergamon, we turned away from grown-up responsibility and ironically complained about our lives in the select company of other overeducated, procrastinating life dodgers until we were spent. Time for bed.

We woke the next morning to blinding brightness and the sound of prayer. It was cathartic to unload, and I felt a little better and more connected to this band of strangers. Aggie and I packed and met the guys again on the roof. We were all smiles over breakfast, although moving a little slowly. We set out early for Pergamon so we could be on the road to Ayvalik around lunchtime.

It was already hot as blazes when we parked the car toward the top of the acropolis. Henry and Aggie went in one direction in search of some ancient theater expert they were assigned to meet with by Turbo. There was some detailed comparison with the theater at Aphrodisias relevant to the book, and anyway, they had a mission. Simon and I agreed to go our separate ways. He had a massive camera and a very specific agenda, and I preferred to walk on my own.

I wandered through a series of temples, palaces, baths, and agora at the very top for the better part of an hour. I stopped a few times to read plaques, but there wasn't too much in English. Suddenly, the site dramatically dropped off toward the theater, and I headed down a steep dirt path. Within thirty seconds, I was suffering from the "jimmy leg" as gravity pulled me down,

down into the bowl. Seventy-eight rows. I remember reading this was the steepest theater in the ancient world and did not doubt it. When I felt like my knees would give out, I took a seat and looked out over the vast valley below. I watched the Italian tourists taking the hill in designer loafers and sandals without breaking a sweat and looked at my filthy sneakers with shame. Time for a cig.

The view was amazing, and I was not anxious to start hiking back up that hill, so I pulled out one of the Japanese ink brushes I bought while traveling there, figuring I'd sketch. Surveying the vastness of this architectural wonder, I settled on a small vignette of some stairs. There was a bit of Greek graffiti carved into the smooth marble. Of course, I couldn't read it. It could have been two years old or almost two thousand years old for all I knew. Maybe it said, "Hail Caesar!" or "Dimitri is a tool." A hot breeze swung the parched grass back and forth as the late morning sun coaxed every possible inch of the ruin out of the shade. Yet, there in a small crack between the engraved letters, a tiny flower pushed defiantly upwards toward the bright white light of the sky. It was an absurdly fearless yet delicate upstart in amazing contrast to the hot, hard, unyielding behemoth from which it sprang. It was struggling to be seen, to thrive, to simply exist. It may have been the most inspiring thing I had seen since my arrival in Turkey and took my breath away.

It was eleven-thirty when I started my hike back up to the parking lot to meet the others. I was huffing and puffing like a woman twice my weight and age. I really needed to reconsider the necessity of cigarettes.

"Right. Let's get on," said Aggie, and we all slid into the hot box. My ass was frying on the cooked Naugahyde. I felt oddly pensive and didn't feel much like chatting, so I rolled down my window and faced the hot wind with my eyes shut. I could feel them all looking at me.

"I'm just a little overheated," I quietly choked out without turning.

We drove for close to an hour, and then we agreed to pull over at a rest stop, where we were most likely to find Western-style toilets as well as refreshments. I peed, bought some water, and stared at the highway, smoking a cigarette in a shady corner away from the pumps. Henry was sent to collect me.

"You okay? You seem a little, well, not yourself today."

"Yeah, sorry, yeah. I'm just a little tired and, like I said, overheated."

"You sure? Pergamon seems to have had an odd effect on you." He smiled.

"Really?" I stamped out my smoke. "Nah. I'm alright. But thanks for caring, Henry." I squeezed his arm a bit, and we walked to the car together. I decided to force myself to perk up. The last thing I wanted was to bring down the group. After all, we only had a couple of days before we were back to the grind... and we were on our way to the piss water 'Amptons.

One and a half hours later, we were off the highway and passing through one tiny village after another. Henry was behind the wheel, sweating and looking shifty. We were lost. Many of the more major turns were roundabouts, and we must have exited too soon or late. Aggie sat cross-armed next to me in the back, her bright red face frowning indignantly. These were the days before navigation or even the printout of Google Maps. Henry had a hand-drawn map and stopped frequently to get directions from the man at the roadside kebab or the guy at the gas station or old men having tea.

We pulled over again, and Simon and I were leaning on the

car in the shade having a smoke while Henry frantically chatted up the guy at the tobacco store. Simon was extolling the virtues of Hendricks Gin versus Bombay Sapphire and Tanqueray. As a lifelong vodka girl, I was intrigued. Suddenly, there was a riot of noise and activity as a horse-drawn cart burst through the adjacent marketplace, followed by a cheering crowd that appeared to include everything with a pulse within fifteen miles.

Atop the cart was a young boy dressed in a white ceremonial costume adorned in silver and gold. On his head was a light blue headpiece, and in his hand, a scepter. He looked like a tiny pope.

"What the...?"

"That sunnae tha is."

"What's sunnae?"

"Nah, SUNNAE," he was chuckling, "Is whe they coot the sken off 'is beets."

My eyes widened. "Ohh! Oh, sure. We call it a bris. Wait. That kid must be eight or nine years old! Yikes."

He was shifting a bit. "Yikes indid."

Henry came out of the tobacco shop with his map just as the crowd dispersed. "What's going on?"

"Sunnae," I said. He looked confused and then understood, looking at Simon. "Ah, Sunnet. Yikes." He was also squirming.

"Yikes," we echoed, laughing. Aggie pulled up in thc car.

"Right, you lot get in. Henry, let Ally ride in front. I've got this in hand."

He was about to resist, but seeing she meant business, climbed in the back with Simon and crumpled up his map. Aggie handed me a small piece of paper with arrows and some words written both in Turkish and in phonetic. She pulled onto the road and headed out of the village.

"Ally, what is the first direction, and which way does the arrow point?"

"It says Muradiye Çarşı Aralığı Sokak, and the arrow points right."

We merged onto a street with that name at the next roundabout and continued on for another twenty minutes with me navigating in marble-mouthed Turkish and Aggie driving while quietly, singing along with the dated disco tunes from the radio. The boys were sulking silently in the back.

Suddenly, the coast appeared on the left. The mood lightened immediately, and we all joined in for the chorus of "Dancing Queen." We were here!

We pulled up to our hotel just before two-thirty. It was near the edge of town but still within walking distance of the many restaurants that lined the pier. The buildings were whitewashed and sun-bleached. It was not elegant, but not devoid of charm. The air was cool and sweet. While this place did not compare with the easy elegance and casual "formality" of the Hamptons, it was a lovely place packed with Turkish families. There was even a quick ferry to a pleasure island nearby where there was a small amusement park. Aggie parked the car without a word and headed for reception to check in. We followed in silence.

Once we were behind the closed door to our room, Aggie finally spoke.

"Sorry I went off. I was just done with driving around and around. Men are stubborn idiots." She was laughing. "Let them think I'm angry and maybe they won't be so quick to take the wheel and shove the women in the back next time."

"As long as you don't look at me. I can't drive stick, remember?"

"It's fine. Let me unpack a bit, and I'll be a pleasure. I don't want to be a damper."

There was a small, shaded courtyard in the rear, and we found the guys there. I was wearing the ridiculous hat again. I was dying to put it on all day, but Henry swore he couldn't see out the rearview mirror. If there was a place in Turkey that could handle this hat, it was Ayvalik.

"Right. Thesa brilliant café a shor walk rie onda wata. We cood doo wif a bite and a caf. If thas ok wif you, Aggie?" He winked. "Nice hat you." He biffed the rim.

"That's enough now. Let's get on." Aggie still had command.

We walked down the street a few blocks past souvenir shops and boat rentals and crossed to the pier. The droves of Turks sitting in cafés and walking flip-flopped with beach paraphernalia were unbent, un-scarved, and unburdened by harsh rural life. Children passed on bikes and scurried with tiny nets to the water's edge to catch small fish and crabs. Others negotiated with their mothers for candy or ice cream from street vendors.

Simon led us to the end of the pier to a busy spot. There was a case piled with fresh seafood just inside. The host waved us in and gestured for us to sit. Simon chose a spot toward the back, open to an unobstructed view of the marina. Before long, I sat with white wine in hand, pulling on one of the last Dunhills and exhaling with gusto into the breeze.

"Anything you recommend, Simon?" Henry asked.

"Aye. Reckon I cud order fer us, if you don mine." He winked again at Aggie.

"Go on then, Simon," Aggie replied. " Ally, do you fancy anything in particular?"

"Actually, if all I ever had was this wine and a cigarette, I'd be perfectly happy forever." I announced dramatically, turning my face to the breeze.

"Ally, that hat suits you," Aggie smiled.

"Thank you, Aggie," I said, eyes closed behind my enormous glasses.

Henry was scanning the menu and finally gave up. "Just order, Simon. You do it well. Ally, would you mind if I bummed a cigarette?"

"Oy, I cud do wif a fag, eh?"

"When in Rome," Aggie added.

They were all looking at me with hands out. I looked at my dwindling supply of Dunhills. Oh well. I guess I could always buy a pack. Did they even sell filtered cigarettes in Turkey? I smiled weakly and pushed the pack across the table.

Another exquisite feast was laid before us thanks to Simon. After our lunch, we quickly threw our beach gear together and loaded back into the car, ladies up front. Simon had already scoped out a restaurant for dinner and was working on selecting an excursion for the following day. He and Henry had collected some brochures while they waited for us and were poring over them in the back as we drove. Letting them pick the boat trip for the next day was the olive branch needed to restore harmony to the group after Aggie temporarily revoked their driving rights.

We decided to forgo an area with many "beach clubs," much to my chagrin, for a quiet sandy beach more known to locals than tourists. The beach was simple and not terribly crowded. There was a small café set back from the shore where we were able to rent sand chairs and a shitty umbrella. I was prepared to skip the rented shade for the benefit of my pale limey pals, but God bless them, they stripped down and greased right up, plopping themselves in the sun facing the water. Between my hat, my glasses, and my natural olive skin, I followed suit with confidence. Poor fair, freckled Henry wrestled with the umbrella behind us.

We sat peacefully for over an hour. Simon listened to his Walkman while Henry and Aggie were reviewing chapter drafts of Turbo's book. I read a Salman Rushdie on the DL, covering the book with my towel. Henry was the first to speak.

"I'm hot. You all want to swim to the moored raft out there?"

I looked over my shades and saw there was a wooden raft structure anchored over fifty feet from the shore.

"Sure. I'm schvitzing. Aggie?"

"In a bit, let me just finish this chapter."

Simon just smiled and nodded without moving. I could hear Duran Duran bleating out "Rio" from his nineties headset. By the time Henry and I reached the water, he was running towards us. We all ran into the shallow water together. The temperature was like piss, and there was not much current, but it was clean, and I could see my feet even as it slowly got deeper. It took a while for the water to reach our middles, and when it did, we started swimming. Aggie caught up, and we all scrambled onto the raft and spread out breathlessly across its slippery surface.

"Oy, thas 'eaven tha is."

"Bloody brilliant," I responded, and we all laughed, lying there until Henry started to freak out. The raft had no shade, and he was frying.

"Too bad Ally couldn't swim out with her bleedin' great hat. There would be shade for the lot of us!" Aggie teased as we jumped into the water for the swim back to shore.

It was a great day. I was truly refreshed. We capped it off

with late-day coffees at the shore café and lazily headed back to the small hotel to clean up for the evening.

Dinner was late that night. After more great seafood and a few bottles of wine, we were really all too wiped to do more than walk around the pleasure island. There were tons of young people, breathless and flushed with excitement, dashing from games to rides. Smiling families walked holding hands, gobbling treats, and carrying tacky prizes. It was quite festive, clean, and wholesome. All I could think was how Americans would ruin this. Like Great Adventure, ruin this.

We were all dozing on the ferry back. That night at the clean, cool, scorpion-free hotel, I slept like a rock for the first time in weeks.

The next morning, we hurried down the pier after a quick breakfast to meet the captain, crew, and passengers already waiting for our day of sailing. We had all overslept a bit.

Apparently, the call to prayer in Ayvalik was not as regular as every other place I'd laid my head since arriving in Turkey. Or maybe the speaker was just more than two feet from my window.

The boat was a good-sized catamaran. I don't know how big that amounts to, but it had two levels, a sizable tanning deck, and enough covered space for all of the Germans aboard to hide after they drank too much at lunch and passed out in the sun. I covered myself in SPF 50 and took my place on the tanning deck next to Aggie, who smartly covered up her limey ass, and Simon, who already had a beer and was working on taking his place with the German lobsters later on. Henry, with his thinning hair and pale freckled skin, was close by, but under cover.

I was pretending to listen to music but was really trying to overhear a conversation between a group of young Germans, who were obviously ethnically Turkish. There were two girls and a boy around twenty. They were clearly talking about me. I felt ridiculously self-conscious. A Jewess in a Muslim country now the subject of gossip amongst the Germans? All of my paranoid conditioning kicked right in. But then I thought I understood them.... "Ist sie Türkin oder Engländerin?" One of the girls asked.

"Sie ist sehr dunkel," said the other girl.

"Die anderen braten," chimed in the dude.

I busted out laughing. All of those years of eavesdropping on my mother and my nanna gossiping in Yiddish had left me with a superficial understanding of German. They were considering if I was also English but decided I was not as I was very dark, and my comrades were literally frying. They looked at me and laughed, too.

"Sie sprechen Deutsch?" the young man asked.

"No, I mean I understand a little."

"Vee spik zum English. Defne, Alara, Ahmet." He pointed to the girls and then himself.

"Aggie, Simon, Henry, and Ally." I replied, pointing to myself and the others.

"Ali is Turkish," Defne said more than asked.

"No, she isn't," I said, smiling.

"We are British," Aggie interjected, gesturing to Simon and herself, "and they are Americans." I was glad she responded and not Simon.

"Your family is not Turkish?" Alara was adding her two cents. "You have a Turkish face and skin."

I was ready to tell them I did not. I had a Jewish face and skin, and they might know more Jews who also looked like me back home if Germany hadn't made that impossible, but I stopped myself. They were not being insulting. They were trying to be friendly, to make a connection. And that was the point of traveling and meeting new people, right?

"Nope. Not a bit Turkish. Do you guys live in Germany?"

"Ja. Born. Ve here for vacation. Visit Turk family. Ze sea." Ahmet nodded toward the water.

We sat with them for the next hour. We all had a beer and talked about the places we had visited. The Germans excitedly spoke of nightclubs and places to party. We learned they were all studying civil engineering back in Munich. We told them about "our" work, and they were very impressed. Then the captain announced that the boat was stopping so we could jump off and swim. The two girls shed their cover-ups and sunglasses and jumped off a narrow ledge on the side of the boat with Ahmet on their heels. The Brits and Henry followed. They bobbed in the water like apples, cheering me off the boat. I had a moment of panic that the water would be frozen, like when I tried surfing off the coast of Portugal. Or maybe there were sharks lurking about, like when I was scuba diving in the open water off the barrier reef in Australia, but I womaned up and took the plunge, shouting with one hand holding my nose and the other holding up my bikini top.

If you are from the New York area and are familiar with its coast, you know it is gorgeous. The tranquility of the dunes peppered with billowing grasses against the contrast of the rhythmic crash of the breaking surf. It is soothing or even meditative. Yet to enter the water any time other than the last two weeks of August is a jarring, full-body slap. However, the Aegean welcomed me into her loving embrace with a therapeutic hug and a warm salty kiss.

Even if she gave me a huge wedgie and nearly made me

guilty of indecent exposure. Piss water 'Amptons indeed.

We frolicked in the sea until the crew called us for lunch. Then we flopped on the deck catching our breath as we dried. The German-Turks joined us for lunch. I insisted we sit under cover given my normally blue friends were now purple from the shoulders up and in complete denial. Simon sat closest to them and chatted them up about the current political climate in Germany. I only caught every third word as their accents made their English difficult to understand, and I had no idea what the hell Simon was saying.

Apparently, droves of Turks came to West Germany in the 1960s and provided cheap labor in a booming post-war economy. Two generations later, they were a well-established minority jockeying for political power commensurate with an ever-improving social status.

Now the Germans were pushing back against them. There was controversy on both sides regarding whether they should be more assimilated or not. There was tension, a group that wanted them deported, yada, yada, the more things change....

After lunch and a few more drinks, the sun caught up with us, and we passed out on the deck. I stretched head to toe next to Henry on a wide bench under cover. Aggie found a spot perpendicular. Simon still chatted with our new friends before knocking off between them in the sun. When we woke, Aggie was horrified. When the boat turned, only was Simon left sleeping in the shade, saving him from further sun damage, but poor, pale Aggie was left exposed. Under the assumption that she would spend the afternoon in the shade, the poor thing neglected to re-apply sunscreen to her salty skin. The worst part was that she slept in an awkward position, exposing her unevenly and leaving her with half a bright red face and two white handprints on her blistering chest. Oy.

When we said goodbye to our new friends, Aggie was almost in tears. Dephne hugged her gently and gave her some aloe as we parted ways.

It was just me and the boys our last night in Ayvalik. Aggie sat weepily submerged in a cool bath in the boys' room and insisted we leave her. So we did. Thanks to Simon, it was another home run of a meal. We killed two bottles of wine and made it an early night. The bright side of poor Aggie's sunburn was that she decided she did not want to stop at a series of old Greek churches abandoned during the population exchange after World War I. I felt a little guilty, but I was relieved.

After dinner, I lay awake until after the last call to prayer, staring at the turning ceiling fan. My toe leisurely scouted the corners of my narrow bed for cool spots. I mulled over everything I saw, everything I was told, and everything I had learned as sleep took me.

I dreamed I was swimming. I couldn't tell if it was Ayvalik or the Hudson River. The water was warm, but there was quite a current. On the shore were my parents and college friends. They weren't even looking at me. So I turned to swim toward a floating platform where the dig crew was smiling and having cocktails. But the current kept pushing me back to land. I was fighting it like mad. I felt I might go under. I thought I heard someone calling out to me... Ally!

I woke up with a start. Aggie was sitting up in bed, crying. "Ally, please, can you get me some more ice? Ugh! This burn is the worst!"

"Sure, Aggie. Sure. Oy. I'm sorry. I'll help you."

She had a rough night but was feeling a little better in the morning. She joined us for breakfast, hat low, glasses on, and chin up.

"So that's a wrap, guys," Henry quipped over his coffee. "I guess once we get back, it is all hands to the pump until the donors' event."

"What is the donors' event?" I asked.

"It's when the dig invites all of the recent large donors and possible future large donors to a little cocktail party at the site, and Dicky and Turbo blow sunshine up their asses and try not to humiliate themselves too much in the process," Henry explained.

"Rob will no doubt be going on about that bleeding book." Sunburn apparently made Aggie a little salty.

"Hey, it's that 'bleeding book' that helps generate the interest that keeps this thing funded and all of us employed."

"No' mey," Simon chimed in. "This me last go. I canna do it nah moe. I canna leave me wee boy agin. Thesa job fo me wiv land surveyers. Construction. Ni Manchester. I'm done afer thes sayson." He had a wistful look in his eyes. "Iss been a good run. Six saysons in all ya know. Cheers to you all." He held up his coffee and we all toasted.

And just like that, my little reprieve was over. We returned the car in Selcuk and grabbed the bus back to the dig. The usual cast was on board, except this time instead of playing surrogate mother to a goat, I was a chaperone to a prize-winning melon. The melon's person eyed me suspiciously for the full two-hour journey. I averted her stare and gazed out the dirty window at the parched landscape peppered by steel stubble and gravel piles.

Eventually, the paved road gave way to dirt roads flanked by fields and the tiny villages they connected. Here stooped figures moved about the fields alongside the slower-moving vehicles. I looked at the women who were likely younger than I and looked older than their years, walking with their children, and was reminded again about the promise I made to Deniz. Somehow, I had to get Kamal to help me. I was not even sure what I could do for this girl with or without his help. Would I be doing her more harm than good giving her a glimpse of a life she might never have? Maybe I was even putting her in danger. One thing was certain. I had taken too much for granted for too long. I had to summon enough courage and gratitude to try and right that.

CHAPTER 9

THE PERFECT STORM

The mini-bus pulled over at the tree-flanked, dirt driveway to our site. I passed the melon to its owner and got out. She gave me a huff and an irritated look. Like I had a nerve not going the full distance of her journey with that fuckin' Jurassic melon on my lap. Henry was already at the back, quickly tossing our bags in the dirt before the driver took off. We collected our stuff and trudged up the dusty road home. It was teatime, and the crew would be assembled in the mess, assuming they were back. The last several days were great. A needed respite from my days in the pit. I felt refreshed and looked forward to catching up with the rest of the group.

Tanya and Philip were already at the table, locked in conversation. I recognized that look on his face. Oy. I wanted to dump my stuff on my bed before grabbing a cup, but there was no way to avoid saying hello as I passed by. This would be good.

"Hi, guys! How was Bodrum and points south?" Their knees were touching below the table. I pretended not to notice.

"Great!" they chimed in unison. "So great," Tanya emphasized, looking Philip in the eyes. I was glad these two saps found each other, really, but I kind of wanted to throw up.

"Awesome. I'll be right back. I just want to toss my stuff on my bed." I moved on as quickly as possible.

The usual suspects were already hosing the dirt. They nodded a hello at me, which I returned, climbing the steps. When I opened the door, Debbie nearly sprang at me.

"Holy shit, Debbie! You scared me. When did you get back?"

"About an hour ago." She looked like she was going to explode. "Oh my God, Ally. I have been dying to tell everyone, but I wanted to tell you first!"

"What, what?" What the hell? She couldn't be pregnant. She wouldn't be that happy.

"Oh my God. Ally. Andrik proposed! We are engaged!"

"Holy shit, Debbie! That is so amazing! Congratulations!" I gave her a huge hug. She was practically jumping up and down. Sure, I thought it sounded a little crazy, but what did I know? Just because I was too irresponsible and self-centered to be in a committed long-term relationship didn't mean everyone else my age was. Wow, what an afternoon.

"Have you made any plans?"

"No, I just told my parents this morning. They think we are nuts." Were they taking a poll?

"No, it's exciting." I wasn't going to yuck her yum. I wondered if she had seen Philip and Tanya. If so, I imagined her too loopy to even notice their new "chemistry." "Are you going to tell everyone?"

"Yeah, I was just hiding out here until I thought they all might be in the mess, so I only had to say it once."

I looked at my watch. "Well, tea is almost over. It's either now, or you hold it in until drinks." She bit her lip thinking it over.

"Okay. Let's go!" She grabbed my hand and dragged me back across the dust to the mess.

Another nod from the three stooges of dirt maintenance. Everyone was catching up. Debbie's eyes surveyed the table to confirm everyone was accounted for. Tanya and Philip were still sitting together, chatting with Henry. Simon, Kamal, and Pano were comparing notes on Bodrum. Kat sat with them but was staring through the mess to the office where Turbo had his arm braced in front of a blistered Aggie, pinning her to a desk. Dicky was nowhere to be found.

"Everyone! I have some news!" Just then a van screeched to a halt in a dust storm in front of the mess, and when the smoke settled, a thirty-something petite woman with a knapsack and what looked like an instrument case was standing in the clear.

"Who is that?" I mouthed to Henry.

"Oh, no," he mouthed back. At that moment, Dicky breezed in.

"I say, Marilyn, is that you? Does Rob know you are here? I don't think he mentioned you were coming."

"Dicky. So nice to see you. No, I'm sure he didn't mention it. Because he didn't know. I wrapped up two weeks early in Białowieża, so I figured I'd hang around here and join the party at the end."

"Aggie, do get Turbo. Aggie! Where the bloody hell is that girl?" Dicky bellowed into his teacup.

"Sorry, Dr. Talbot. I'm just here. What can I do for you?"

We were all staring, a dumbstruck audience for this weird show.

"Aggie, where's Turbo?"

"He's in the office, Dr. Talbot."

"Well, go on. Get him, for God's sake. His bloody wife is here. Waiting. I dare say the poor woman will drop dead of heatstroke, so do get on! And what's wrong with your face?" I couldn't help but glance toward Kat. She was looking at her feet. Now she knew for sure there was no chance. Turbo came bursting out of the screen door. He looked as shocked as the rest of us.

"Marilyn? My God!" There were hugs and kisses. He picked up the case. "Why didn't you say you were coming? What happened?"

"Well, it was a perfect year for owls, and I got all of the photos I needed for my book much faster than I thought. So, I cut the season short... figured I'd pop down and surprise you. Been ages since I could make the season." Well, Turbo's grab-ass season was certainly being cut short.

"Come, let me help you get settled. You're on the late side for tea..."

"Never mind. I want to get cleaned up before cocktails." The couple walked off to Turbo's cabin. We were all still just staring, mouths agape. Aggie was the only one smiling. It was dead silent. I looked back at Debbie, who was looking at me, shaking her head. I guess she wanted to hold off now. I didn't blame her. I created a diversion.

"Kamal, Tanya, you guys up for a run?" Tanya looked at Philip. "No thanks," Tanya quickly refused.

"Sure," answered Kamal, looking back at Tanya.

"Do you mind running into Geyre with me? I want to grab a few packs of cigarettes. My travel companions cleaned me out."

"No prob." He really did have a beautiful smile.

"Great. Well then, I will just change."

"I'm gonna write a letter, so I'll walk back with you," Debbie added, scrambling to her feet. The group dispersed, and I walked back to the bunk with Debbie to change.

"Thanks for that," said Debbie, flopping down on her cot. "I didn't want to say it just then. Such a weird moment." She nibbled a cuticle.

"I know. Do you think he was happy to see her? I mean Turbo."

"Not likely. But I bet Aggie was," she laughed.

"He is not subtle. What is the deal there? I thought she was carrying a trumpet."

Debbie snapped back to herself and started dishing. "Well, Marilyn is an ornithologist. That case is for her camera. She is always traveling the world photographing birds for this book or that article. Pretty much leaves Turbo to do as he pleases, if you know what I mean. But I think she is clueless. Anyway, Aggie may have been happy to see her, but Kat certainly wasn't. She looked like her head was going to explode."

"Yeah. Come to think of it, Tanya looked weird, too. She usually jumps on any opportunity to be next to Kamal." I was feeling her out to see if she picked up on the vibe between Philip and Tanya.

"Seriously. Hey, grab me a pack of Parliaments, please." If she thought those two were screwing around, she gave no hint.

I met up with Kamal in front of the mess. He was stretching and double-knotting his sneakers. I couldn't help myself. I tried to look up his shorts. "Ready?"

We had to cut through the Agora to the road that led to Geyre. I was a good twenty feet behind him most of the time. The foam covers of my headphones were soaked in sweat. I felt extremely self-conscious again in my running shorts and tank amongst the covered heads, arms, and legs of the village, but in those days, I was willing to risk a public stoning for a pack of smokes. Regardless, I had Kamal to protect me.

We went into the "tütün dükkanı," tobacco shop, and I stood like a mute as Kamal spoke to the clerk. I produced some wet bills from my sock to pay and was treated to a look of pure disgust from the clerk. Can't say I blamed him there. Tempted as I was to light up immediately, I thought it best to restrain myself until we were back at camp. I shoved the boxes in my soaked jogging bra and headed for the door.

When we were back on the street, I noticed Deniz looking my way and then dodging behind a fruit cart to avoid meeting up with us. Kamal looked at me and asked, "Do you feel like walking back? I've kind of had it today."

I was pretty sure he saw the shape I was in and was cutting me a break, but whatever. "Sure. No problem." I wished I had bought a bottle of water. This was the first time I could recall being alone with Kamal. On top of being adorable, I thought he was very personable, and unlike so many on this dig, seemed to have no agenda.

"Did you notice a weird vibe in the mess after tea?" Okay, so maybe he was a gossip, but nobody is perfect.

"Well, yeah, Kamal. I think Turbo's wife's dramatic entrance left us all a little stunned." I chuckled.

"No. I mean before that. Like, Tanya and Philip?"

"Well, I don't know. What do you mean?" I was fishing. So, shoot me.

"I was talking to Pano, who was with them, when I got back. He said they hooked up in Bodrum." Kamal, you little yenta. He kept going. "Well, I don't know if you know, but last year Tanya and I were kind of together." Yeah, I knew. "Anyway, it has been so weird this season between us, with me being married and all...." He trailed off and stopped walking. He was looking right at me right now. "I think she was really upset. I don't know what I'm trying to say and why I am telling you this, Ally. I'm sorry." He looked past me.

"No, it is fine. I—there is a lot going on. Here, I mean. I'm sorry. I am trying to keep my head down."

"Yeah. Well, I think her feelings were different from mine, even last summer, and, well, I didn't mention Lisa, my wife, during the year, because I well, I didn't know how to—"

I cut him off. "Kamal, this is really none of my business, but don't beat yourself up. Tanya isn't the first person to read too much into a little summer fun. And you're not the first person to move on from a casual thing without permission. Shit happens. People's feelings get hurt. She'll get over it. And if what you say is true, she is doing her best."

"Thanks, Ally. I thought you of everyone would understand."

"Yeah...wait, what? What do you mean?" He knew he just stepped in it.

"Ugh. Well, Philip and you, well, right? Weren't you...? Ugh."

I was fuming. "Look. We were friends... for a long time. He had another girlfriend like forever, I had other entanglements, and we were friends. Then we were both free and met up one night with a few people in The City over Thanksgiving break, and we all had too much to drink and that was that. We crossed the line. And it was weird. We spent a month together back at school in the chaos just before Christmas as kind of a couple but it wasn't right, and that was that. What did he tell you, Kamal? Really."

He was squirming. "Well, it wasn't really me. He kind of told Tanya and she told me."

"Again, please, what did he say?"

"Well, he was sitting with Tanya and Jeff and kind of said that you were a little heartless. That you hung out with him and tossed him when you were bored and that you did the same thing to another guy in your class."

"That is bullshit!" I was practically yelling at him. "Why is it when a guy and a girl hang out casually and she decides it's run its course before he does, she is vilified for it? I don't see anyone giving you shit for moving on after Tanya. I'm a fucking twenty-six-year-old woman. Consenting adults!"

"Okay. Calm down." He was laughing. "Don't shoot the messenger." His English was very good. "But you get my point. Sometimes you do people you can't undo." Okay, not that good.

"I'm sorry, Kamal. I got angry because I feel guilty, and I am really fuckin' sick of feeling guilty. I am sick of apologizing for my choices. All of them. This wasn't a big deal. At least, I didn't think it was. And I don't appreciate him badmouthing me. I'm done feeling bad now."

"Me too!" He was still chuckling.

"I mean, I don't see anyone badmouthing Andrik for moving on. And he was serious with Nina. And now he and Debbie are..." I caught myself. "...getting serious."

We looked at each other for another second and then turned and walked back to camp, chit-chatting about this and that. I told him about my family and our latest addition. He told me about his. He mentioned that his sister Ayeleen was trying to transfer to Miami University to live with him and Lisa. His parents wanted her to leave Turkey. Apparently, in recent years, there was a strong conservative Turkish movement that wanted to undo some of the social progress brought on by a more secularized Turkey. Kamal's parents were worried that extremists could really take control of the government and restrict women's rights and force religious rules of modesty, etc. on the entire population. I got it. He said everything without saying it. He married an American not only to keep himself in the US but also to help his sister. We were back in front of the mess now. Everyone was gone. I looked at him.

"I understand. I hope Ayeleen can leave and stay with you, both of you. There is nothing more important than family." He nodded, and we went our separate ways. His secret was safe with me. This was bigger than who was screwing whom. This was Ayeleen's future. I thought about the opportunities I took for granted as an American woman and what people around the world were willing to risk to share them.

CHAPTER 10

MORE LAYERS

I was still thinking about what Kamal was doing for his sister when I got back to the bunk. Debbie was literally waiting to pounce on me.

"You didn't tell him, did you?"

"No, Debbie. We were running, not talking. You know I'm not in that kind of shape."

"Well then at the end. I saw you guys walking back. I saw you talking." She seemed to be unraveling. I think the pressure of her news was backing up on her, and if she didn't let it go, it was going to get ugly.

"No, Debbie. We were talking about something else. Nothing." I changed the subject. "So, you should make your announcement at cocktails. That would be festive. Or dinner." She considered this.

"Yeah. You're right." That seemed to chill her out.

Later at cocktails, Dicky was talking too loudly to Kat, who wasn't listening but was instead staring daggers at Turbo and the lovely Marilyn. Simon, Aggie, and Pano were arguing about soccer. (No, sorry, I am an American, and I will not call it football.) We were still missing Philip and Tanya. Debbie had that look of a paranoid pothead. Like she was the only one high at the bar and thought everyone was looking at her. Then Philip and Tanya walked in, fixing their hair and brushing dirt off their shoulders. Gross. Debbie jumped up and was about to start when Turbo interrupted her.

"Oh, good you are all here. Big news. I got confirmation today that *Life Magazine* will be doing a special feature on the dig next month. It is a huge PR plug for the foundation. They will be here a few days in the next week or so and will circle back for the patrons' dinner. They will be interviewing many of you guys in the field and around camp. Keep in mind, this is a national publication, and a great article will mean a lot of press and money for the work. No pressure." He winked and looked at the pocket watch pulled from the depths of a cargo pocket just as Deniz hit the pan. "Oh, dinner time already. Let's go!" I looked at Debbie's face. If she didn't say it soon, I was afraid she'd pass out. I locked arms with her and dragged her toward the mess.

We were all seated. Kofte with rice was placed in front of us. Debbie stood up. "Everyone. I have good news!"

"Yeah, we know." Philip interrupted, "There is baklava. I saw Ally headed for the kitchen half naked." Dick. I prepared to eviscerate him, but Debbie interrupted, yelling.

"No! God dammit! I am getting married! Andrik proposed over the break, and we are getting married!" Everyone was stunned and silent. I think equally from the news and how it was delivered. Debbie was panting. I tried to save the moment.

"That is amazing! Isn't that amazing? We should make a toast!" I jumped up and raised my glass, which was water. The crowd stood, too, and toasted Debbie and Andrik with whatever they were drinking. Everyone congratulated and hugged her.

Just as we were all settling back down, Dicky staggered out of the office. Ugh. He had missed the announcement. We would have to do it again.

“Right then. What is all the fuss?”

“Debbie and Andrik are getting married!” Aggie gushed.

“Who the bloody hell is Debbie? Oh, right. Well, on your own head be it! Did I hear there was baklava? Well done, Ally.” He leered at me knowingly. And with that, we all sat down for dinner.

After dinner, I took advantage of Tanya’s new fixation with Philip to get near Kamal and ask if he would help me translate for Deniz’s sister. I found him reading in the lounge.

“So, Kamal, I have a weird question for you. The guy with the baklava, Deniz? He has a sister, Akara. She is really interested in buildings or architecture. Actually, I am not exactly sure what she is interested in. Deniz’s English isn’t so great.”

“Yeah? So how can I help?” He was eying me suspiciously.

“Well, I told him I would talk with her. He asked me to. Only she doesn’t speak much English.”

“Talk with her about what?”

“Honestly, I am not sure,” I laughed nervously. “Anyway, she wants to ask questions or have discussions about buildings. I asked why she couldn’t speak with you, but it is apparently forbidden for her to have a conversation with a man.” That got a raised eyebrow. “So I thought you could translate and maybe prevent me from making any major Turkish social faux pas and avert an international incident.”

“You got that right. These people are very backward. I cannot meet her alone. I get you mean well, Ally, but what do you expect to do for this girl? If her parents, her father, do not want her to be educated, she won't be. Making her more willful and headstrong will not serve her. You may be helping her to become an outcast in her own community thus worsening her prospects."

"I…I hadn't thought of that."

"I know being American makes it difficult for you to see the world through a less than egalitarian lens, but this is a different culture."

I was annoyed considering what he was doing for his sister. "I know. I get it, but it was her brother who came to me. I didn't volunteer. So she is getting some support. Really, I thought you of all people would understand. Just because she is poor doesn't mean she shouldn't have hope."

He exhaled deeply and looked down at his feet before responding. "Yeah. Yeah, you are right. Again, I do not think we can help her. But we can try. At least broaden her horizons a bit. Tell him to bring her tomorrow. We can cut tea short and meet in the baths. No one can know. For her sake, got it?"

"Thank you, Kamal. Thank you so much!" I stopped in the kitchen to tell Deniz on my way to change. I saw Philip watching me as he crossed the lounge with Tanya shaking his head. Fuck him and his assumptions. I was on a mission.

That night I dreamed I was in the Fugees' video for "Ready or Not." You know the one… they are running through drainpipes and trying to escape some kind of attack in the desert, on jet skis, and in the jungle all at the same time. Anyway, somehow, I was Lauryn Hill. I wasn't singing, but the music was playing. I executed the rescue of a young girl from a cell and took off with her on my motorcycle. Angry men are in hot pursuit as we sprint across a beach. We jump to a chopper, and I pull her up, taking the controls and lifting off the ground as a mob of angry men burst out of the jungle and wave their angry fists at us. My dad was leading them.

When he opened his mouth to yell, the first call to prayer pulled me from the scene and back to my sweaty cot.

I looked over to Debbie. She was saying "fuck it" to the doubters and following her truth. She was the brave one. Not me. If that poor girl Akara knew what a hypocrite she had hitched her wagon to, she'd be looking for another tow. I lay sweating in the dawn light, reflecting on the irony.

The next morning at breakfast, Deniz gave me a knowing nod, unfortunately witnessed by Philip. Oy. That was all he needed. He rolled his eyes with a half-sneer, and before I could attempt to defend my virtue, Debbie grabbed me to walk in the already oppressive heat to our hole ground. She chattered excitedly about her call with Andrik. She was positively effervescent. They would return to the US and plan a wedding with their families for next spring. Secretly, they were also planning a romantic private ceremony on a cliff somewhere in the Greek islands after the dig. They would be secretly married. I envied her guts. Neither of their parents were thrilled by their news, and but the couple were giving zero fucks. Sink or swim, they were taking control of their lives as well as responsibility for their actions.

Maybe that was what I really envied. Maybe I wasn't so much stifled by my parents' disapproval as by my inexplicable need for their praise. Why? Did their affirmation of me, of my choices, somehow lessen my responsibility for their outcomes? Was I using them as a crutch to shoulder the burden of taking control of my life? Of... being an adult? Shit, that was sobering.

That night, instead of our usual run, Kamal and I headed straight to the baths to meet Deniz and Akara. It was awkward.

Akara could barely look up, and she didn't even acknowledge Kamal. Deniz gestured for us to sit. He had to run some kitchen errands in town but would be back in an hour. Akara nodded, barely looking up from her shoes. I put my hand on her back and led her to a shaded spot. Kamal followed. When we were seated, I asked her how I could help her. What she wanted to know. She looked at my face and started speaking quietly. Kamal translated.

"She wants to know why we come here. What we are looking for." She waved her hands to indicate the site. "She wants to know who built this place and when."

"The Greeks built it. Tell her. When they were under the Romans. You know. Tell her about Aphrodite and the sculpture...." Kamal asked her something in Turkish, and she nodded.

"What did you ask her?"

"I asked if she could read. She can. Apparently, the locals don't talk much about the place. Maybe we could give her some books? Then we can discuss them with her. I don't think she is so much interested in architecture as in archeology. Specifically, this site, given that it is a mystery right under her nose." He started to explain some things to her in Turkish. She was nodding enthusiastically, but still not looking at him. I felt a little extraneous, but knowing this conversation could not happen without my chaperone, so to speak, made me feel better. The hour flew by, and Deniz was back to collect her. They were both all smiles and thank you's as they hurried back to the village.

When we left Deniz and Akara, we were cutting it fine to be back in time to shower up for dinner. Kamal suggested we jog back to camp. He knew a shortcut through a less traveled bit of the site. It was a little hilly and rocky but more shaded, mercifully. I was trying to keep up with him, but shit, he was fast. It was no chore to be behind him. This kid had an ass. Maybe I should have been paying less attention to it because I tripped on a root or a rock or whatever and twisted my ankle. I went down with a yelp. Kamal stopped dead in his tracks.

"Ally, you okay? Shit! What happened?"

"I twisted my ankle. It is fine. I'll be fine. I just need to sit a minute. And to walk back.

You don't have to wait." I could see the site buildings in the distance. I could find my way.

"Don't worry. I won't leave you. For fear of goat attack. Let me see." He sat next to me, close in the dirt. He took my leg in his lap and inspected it for damage. I winced, wishing I had shaved more recently.

"I think you will live." He was rubbing the sore spot, smiling. Damn, that felt good. For a second, I was imagining those hands... in other places. But Kamal was staring at me.

"Ally, even if there is no big outcome, what you are trying to do for Akara is very generous."

"No. It is nothing. Really. Why wouldn't I help her?"

"The dig has been here for twenty years. The people associated with it are not so well regarded in the town. Not trusted. Something about you made Deniz feel he could come to you."

"Well, he doesn't even know me. Except that I have a sweet tooth." I laughed nervously. The way he was looking at me... with those hazel-green eyes and black, fluttery full lashes. Why had I never noticed those lashes?

"You are an honest person, Ally. You seem very comfortable in your skin, and because of that, you don't make other people feel small. These intellectuals are always trying to make everything, themselves, all this so important that it can make these regular people feel invisible. This is their home, and they feel unwelcome. You don't make people feel that way. That is why he came to you. He knew you wouldn't treat him like dirt." I felt guilty now for thinking Deniz was a sex offender.

"I don't feel so comfortable sometimes. Sometimes I just feel lost." My voice broke.

"But you can admit it. Most people can't. You are very real." He paused, his lip taking a half-wicked turn up. "And very sexy." Shut. The. Front. Door. His face was close to mine now. I could feel his breath. I swear I could practically feel those lashes fluttering on my cheek. His tanned knee was touching mine, and he casually reached out to tuck a loose strand of my gross hair behind my sweaty ear. His hand lingered on my neck. He didn't draw me toward him. He was waiting for me to make the next move. God, even sweaty, he smelled good. Now, I have kissed plenty of people's friends, brothers, even other people's boyfriends along the way, but I have never kissed someone's husband. Even a pretend husband. That was a line. I snapped out of it and pulled back. He knew immediately he had miscalculated.

"Ally, I am so sorry. I just... I am so embarrassed. Please... I am not an asshole. I just really like you. And I think you understand the truth of my situation. I'm pretty sure everyone knows. Oh God, I am an asshole."

"It's okay. I am flattered, really." I was scrambling to my feet. "I just can't. Not with your 'situation,' and I really don't want to give Philip any more ammunition. I'm pretty sure he is spreading a rumor that I am giving it to Deniz to get baklava."

"You don't have to explain. I shouldn't have put you in that position. I agree. The group has big eyes and bigger mouths. I had no right to involve you in my mess. Besides, any hint that the marriage is less than one hundred percent legit and I could get in real trouble. Legal trouble. And Philip is a pussy, by the way. What the hell were you thinking?" He was laughing. Then I was.

"Not every idea is a good one. What can I say? Idle hands." I shrugged and then smiled at him. "Friends then? I could use one."

"Friends. Although you don't make it easy. Let me at least help you back on that ankle." He winked, holding out his hand.

"I think I can manage." We walked back to the site talking casually as if nothing had happened.

Of course, Philip and Tanya were sitting in the dining room as we passed by. They exchanged knowing glances as Kamal and I passed, heading back to our respective bunks, and I swear I almost punched Philip's fucking face. I passed the office and could see Turbo lecherously leaning over Aggie at her computer. I rapped on the door, sending him across the room, and stuck my head in.

"Aggie, there you are. I think Kat is looking for you. She is with the others getting a jump-start on cocktails in the lounge." She heaved a sigh of relief and leapt to her feet, squeezing my arm as she rushed past me and out the door. I smiled at Turbo and marched toward the stairs of my cabin with my head held high.

When I opened the door, Debbie was sprawled out reading a letter, frowning.

"Andrik was supposed to come in a couple of weeks for a visit, but he is staying in Greece." She pouted and sighed. "Though he says he is still coming for the donor party." She perked up a bit.

"That's exciting." I was still stewing over Philip and Turbo.

Turbo's wife resurfaced at dinner that evening, and his mood was quite reserved. Tanya and Philip paired up next to Turbo, with Aggie as far from them as possible. Her face was now shedding its sun-burnt skin, and she looked like she just had a chemical peel. Kamal sat to her left, Debbie on her right, and me in the middle. Everyone was quiet. Then Dicky burst through the mesh flaps, tearing one and practically face-planting. Apparently, not everyone missed cocktails.

"Bloody hell. Aggie, be a luv and tell someone about that. Right, so what's for dinner?"

"Maybe Ally could flit by the kitchen and drum up something good," Philip drawled under his breath.

"What was that, Philip? Did you say something?" I was staring him down as Deniz and the crew swept in with trays of stew and rice. Dinner began in silence, broken only when a van slowed in front of the mess, bringing with it a cloud of dust that enveloped us as we ate. Two men emerged from the cloud and headed our way, the younger one in front, smiling. The other, a middle-aged man, slinked miserably a few steps behind him.

The young guy gave Turbo a bro hug and backslap. To Dicky, he gave a half-nodded "S'up?" Great. A dude.

"Fedder, just in time for dinner," Turbo started. "Is that Gonzalos with you?" He jerked his head in the direction of the man standing ten feet away with all of their bags and equipment.

"Yeah. He is a little worse for wear. We had an epic night in Istanbul, and the drive from the airport in Izmir was a little... shitty."

"Very eloquent for a member of the press," Turbo joked.

"Anyway, let me introduce you to the crew, and then you can get settled. I'll tell the boys in the kitchen to leave you guys a plate if you feel up to it."

Rob stood in front of us with his hand on the dude's back. "Everyone. Can I please have your attention? This is Todd Fedder. He is the reporter from Life Magazine. The gentleman behind us is Gonzolez. His photographer." The photographer scoffed a bit. "They will be with us for a few days taking photographs and interviewing a few of you. Just go about your business naturally but answer any questions they have."

"You won't even know we are here." Fedder grinned cockily and quickly scanned all of our faces.

"Henry and Pano, why don't you give them a hand with their stuff and show them to cabin four? That one has a ceiling fan." Turbo winked at Fedder. Wait, what? Some of these shit shacks had fans? "Henry, stop in the kitchen on your way back and tell Deniz to leave them some food."

Henry and Pano jumped up and grabbed two armfuls each and moved quickly toward the bunks, eager to get back to their dinners. Gonzalez grabbed the rest and followed. Fedder carried nothing except his jacket thrown over one shoulder. He sauntered after them with a nod toward Turbo.

"Well, everyone," Turbo addressed us after they were out of earshot, "Fedder, Todd, is an old pal of mine and as smart as they come. Please be cooperative in any way you can be. As I mentioned, this could be a huge boon for our interests." He paused, "But exercise discretion with regard to matters not relevant to the dig." His eyes inadvertently shifted toward Dicky and back to us. "Fedder started his career writing gossip pieces for Page Six of the *Post*, and well, old habits."

He sat back down and resumed eating. Marilyn was

chatting with Dicky, who seemed completely unfazed by the arrival of the press.

After dessert, I headed back toward my cabin to get some stationery for a letter. I needed to fill Mel in on Debbie's engagement, Kamal's pass, and all other matters of vital importance. I was intercepted by Fedder, who seemed a little lost. He had a too-small towel wrapped around his slim waist, and his bare chest was covered with the same thick, dark hair that covered his head.

"Hey. I was hoping you could help me get cleaned up." He was twirling his dark chest hair and grinning. Gross. "You know, show me where the showers are."

"Uh. Yeah. Sure. This way," I stammered. He was eying me like a cartoon dog looking at a steak. I walked ahead of him and pointed to the shower house. He made my skin crawl. "There. Next to the toilets." I gestured toward the shower building and backed away a little so I could make my escape.

"Thank you. And you are?"

"Ally. Ally Acker." Another step back. He reached out to shake my hand, forcing me to step forward a bit to take it.

"Todd Fedder." He held onto my hand for a few seconds too long. "Well, Ally Acker. I'm hoping maybe you could spend some time with me. Talking about the work here. Maybe tomorrow?" He was grinning like the Cheshire Cat.

"Yeah. Well, sure. Rob, Dr. Turbo, requested we answer any of your questions. I am not an expert. It is my first year. You'd be better off with one of the PhDs. But feel free to catch up with me at breakfast if it will help." Rather than in the studio after noon. More witnesses. "Goodnight, then." I nodded curtly and turned to walk away.

"Goodnight, then, Ally Acker." He said my name like it was

laced with innuendo. Like it was Yiddish for blow job. Another detail to include in my letter to Mel.

I had a restless night's sleep after writing my letter. I passed out before Debbie came back in but was up after the last call to prayer and could not get back to sleep. I kept thinking about that predator in cabin four. I assumed him to be sleeping soundly and comfortably cool thanks to the secret fan. What a creep. I needed to give Debbie and the other girls a heads up to steer clear of him.

My mind was racing as I stared at the ceiling, watching an imaginary fan turning and turning. I thought about Philip and how he continued to punish me for wounding his ego, even though he apparently moved on. Eventually I drifted off and dreamed.

I was in the shower. I stood with my eyes closed, the water beating me on the face. I wasn't washing or rinsing. Just standing there being pummeled by the stream. I was in no hurry to get out of the shower. There was someone in my apartment I did not want to face. Was it Philip? My parents? Creepy Fedder? I wasn't sure if I was scared or just procrastinating. I was never getting out of that shower. The water sputtered, hissing and spitting angrily. I swept my hands over my face, wiping the shower spray out of my eyes, but I could hear someone yelling my name, muffled by the shower. "Allau!"

When the five a.m. call to prayer woke me, I shot straight up in bed to find a feral cat inches from my face. It clung to the towel over my head, meowing angrily and spitting at me. I screamed, waking Debbie, who saw the cat and ran from the cabin, shrieking, "I'm allergic!"

I met her on the stairs, panting and laughing. "Oh my God, oh my God! Where did that thing come from?" I could barely breathe.

"The kitchens, I'd guess. How the hell are we getting it out of there?" She had her hand on her chest. "I am really allergic."

"And they say I'm high maintenance? Don't sweat it. I'll get a snack and lure it out."

Deniz was there already, prepping for breakfast. He gave me a piece of cheese on a plate and confirmed our date to meet with Akara again later in the week. I thanked him and headed back to lay my trap. Wouldn't you know it, son-of-a-bitch Philip saw me coming from the kitchen in my PJ's and bidding farewell to Deniz. He ducked back into his cabin before I could say a word. Really, I could not get a break.

Debbie and I put the plate on the steps to our bunk and left the door propped open with a shoe while we washed. By the time we came back, we seemed to be cat-free. We dressed and headed to the mess for breakfast.

Fedder reared his ugly head just as we were heading out to the field. He was chatting with Turbo and drinking from a to-go cup. He nodded a s'up in my direction. I grabbed my bag and scooted out of the mess before he could snag me. Gonzalez was nowhere to be found. Maybe if he had to wait for him, I would get a solid head start and he wouldn't find me.

No such luck. I was stationed on my wall. Debbie was in sight but a good fifty feet away, showing her team where to dig. I was so focused on my rocks, my headphones blasting Marley, I didn't even see him come up behind me until his shadow overtook mine. I was knocked off balance by surprise and stumbled a bit. He grabbed me around the waist.

"Oh God! You made me jump, Mr. Fedder. I—I almost fell off." I steadied myself and took a step away from him, holding my clipboard at ninety degrees to my body to at least maintain that distance.

"You're alright. And it's Todd." He looked me up and down, smirking.

"Right. Todd. Uhh. How can I help you?"

"I was hoping we could chat. Maybe you could help me with my article. Maybe I could help you." He was inching towards me. Like a tiger stalking his kill.

"Well, I uhh, I am not your best resource. Really. Like I said, I just graduated from architecture school. I am not a seasoned expert. You are best off talking with Debbie or Henry. Or both. They have spent several seasons here and can give you the experienced perspective of both an archeologist as well as an architectural historian." I was babbling and stepping back as he continued, slowly moving toward me. Then he stopped, pinching my clipboard as if to say "Gotcha."

"I heard you had a treat this morning." He teased me, adjusting his Mets cap on his thick, curly hair. My face screwed up in confusion. "Waking up with a pussy in my face is my favorite way to start the day." Gross. I did not know what to say. Where to go. I was frozen like a deer in headlights. I was accustomed to my guy friends making bawdy comments in my presence. A lot of "that's what she said" kind of humor. I was no prude and could be vulgar with the best of them. But this? This was blatant harassment, and it was new to me. How was I getting out of this with my clothes on? Did I smack this guy or just play it off and avoid him for the next couple of days? Did I tell Turbo? I thought I heard him say these guys were leaving Friday night. That left three more days.

"Ally! Ally! Oh, there you are. Ally, it is lunchtime. Let's go!" Debbie saved me.

Thank God.

"Yeah. Thank you, Debbie! Yes. Lunchtime. Mr. Fedder, Todd, let me show you the way back." I turned and jumped down off the wall. Debbie waited for us both, and we all headed back together. Fedder asked her a lot of questions and recorded her responses on a small device he pulled from his vest. I walked silently in their company, my head reeling. I had to figure out a way to deal with this, or at least to artfully avoid dealing with it.

As we were well beyond the halfway point in the season, my time would now be split. In the morning, I would be with Debbie, completing the field drawings of the monument walls, and after rest time, I would work on transcribing all of my field sketches to ink on mylar. As a lefty, my ink skills have never been a strength. Right-handed people do not understand the extent to which the world is constructed to suit them. Mylar sheets are generally attached to a drawing board or a table with a Mayline device. A Mayline is the brand name for a particular straight edge fastened to a flat surface which can move up and down a page on a pair of thin cables to create straight lines or limitless different angles if used in conjunction with an adjustable triangle. A left-handed person's drawing hand has to technically pass over the wet ink as it moves left to right... as we are taught to write as well as draw in the West. The page must be secured to the table straight. Not tilted as a lefty might turn a notebook to write. So a lefty might train herself to work right to left when inking to avoid making a mess. This involves a lot of mental back and forth since we read and write left to right. I have often wondered if God was a lefty since many of the early languages, including Hebrew and Aramaic, were written right to left. If so, She really wouldn't appreciate the current state of things. Anyway, I just had to take my time and concentrate. I was skipping rest after lunch to give myself some extra time.

With Akara's lessons eating into my free time, it was all I could spare. Henry found me in the studio right after lunch the next day.

"You're an eager beaver."

"Really. I need a little extra time. Lefty."

He was smiling. "Did you get cornered by the press yet?"

"God no," I lied. I wasn't sure what he meant by cornered, and I had no intention of telling him about my morning. "As the only newbie on this dig, I've been trying to avoid them. Whatever I say, I will end up sounding like an idiot."

"Don't be so hard on yourself. You may not be an academic, but you are also not promoting anything. They might prefer someone who answers the questions they want to ask or gives them a more personal take. Something they can really grab onto."

"That's kind of what I'm afraid of."

He clamped on his headphones, chuckling, and he locked in on his work.

Kamal and I met with Akara again on Thursday. She had so many questions about the site and other sites in general. Again, this was '98. No smartphones and not much of an internet yet to research, even if she could get her hands on a computer. The village did not boast much of a library. Given the very traditional and conservative values in her community, her intellectual curiosity might not have been enthusiastically received. She would barely look at Kamal. She posed her questions to me. He would answer, and she would either look at me or her shoes, nodding. I sat there smiling like an idiot.

We were jogging back to the site when Kamal slowed to a walk ahead of me so I could catch up.

"I was thinking." He was barely breathing hard.

"Yeah, 'bout what?" I could barely sputter out without coughing up a lung. Damn Dunhills.

"I have several Turkish books about this site, plus several others at my parents' place. Books I'll never read again. I doubt I'll ever be taking them with me wherever I end up. Maybe I could give them to Akara?"

"That's really generous. I'm sure she would love that."

"I'm going there this weekend. Maybe you want to come?"

"Kamal. I—I am sorry. I thought we...."

"Ally, no. I mean I invited Debbie and Simon as well while you were in the studio. I forgot to mention it. My sister will be there, too, with a friend. You are perfectly safe." He grinned.

"Oh. Sure!" I blushed like a sixteen year old. Ugh. "That is so nice of you. And your parents don't mind?"

"No. It is a big enough place. They are retired. They live there all summer. We usually head out as soon as we can get cleaned up on Saturday evening. It's about a two-hour drive. We miss dinner, but my mother lays out enough food for a dozen men. Sunday, we spend time on the beach and then head back again after dinner."

"Sounds like a plan. Thank you!"

"My pleasure." He winked. Is it possible Kamal was truly a genuinely nice guy? Was he just trying to be kind to me, Akara, Debbie, and Simon for that matter? No ulterior motive? Regardless, it probably wouldn't look great to those who wanted to believe otherwise. Screw it. I wanted to eat something good and sleep in a clean bed. So I was in.

Back in the bunk, Debbie grabbed me.

"So, you and I off to Kamal's Saturday?" She was just getting started.

"Yeah, he mentioned it. Sounds like fun! I really have to

buckle down on my inking, but...." She cut me off.

"Yeah, too bad Andrik won't be around, or the four of us could all hang out together, you know what I mean?"

I was pissed. "Yes, Debbie. I do know what you mean, but not what you are talking about. We are just—"

"Well, Philip said—"

"I don't give a shit what Philip said. He has a lot of nerve."

"Well, you have been spending a lot of time together. And Tanya..."

"Tanya and Philip both should stop taking their own feelings of rejection out on me. Not to mention it is bullshit that could actually hurt people who matter more than I do if anyone believes what Tanya is insinuating. Maybe she can't imagine not flinging herself at him if given the chance, but that is not my problem."

"I'm sorry, Ally..."

I was storming to the shower, and of course, there was Kamal.

"Hey, Ally, what's wrong?" And ugh, there was Philip coming out right behind him with a shit-eating grin.

"Hi, Kamal. Nothing really. Thank you." I managed quietly. I looked Philip right in his smirking face as I brushed past. "Go fuck yourself, Philip." I snapped as the screen door slammed shut behind me.

The shower cleared my head and calmed me down. By the time I was peeking my head out, Deniz was hosing down the dirt. He was right in my path. I was not in the mood to engage, so I gave him a nod, which he returned smiling broadly as Dicky passed, obviously making note of the exchange. "So, baklava again, is it? Well done, Ally. Cheers!"

You know it is bad enough to be the subject of gossip, but

to not even be guilty of any of the fun in question? Unacceptable.

I was relieved that Debbie headed out before I got back. I needed to get changed quickly and see if I could get a few minutes of ink work in before dinner. My path to the studio was clear, thankfully, but I did see Fedder had Kat cornered in the lounge, or maybe it was the other way around. All the more reason to skip cocktails.

I had on my huge headphones but was not playing any music. I wanted to avoid chit-chat and still be able to hear anyone who might turn up. Nothing says "Do not disturb" like big, stupid headphones.

I heard Turbo arguing with a woman I was pretty sure was his wife. Something about her being disappointed that he couldn't at least carry on discreetly like an adult scumbag. She would make sure that "little crumpet" never crossed the pond. Yikes.

I was quiet all through dinner that night, trying to keep a low profile. Fedder continued to chat up Kat, making little notes in a black journal throughout dinner. He saw me notice and winked at me. Yuck.

After dinner, Turbo suggested escorting Fedder and Gonzalez around the site for an evening tour, although the latter had missed dinner and was nowhere to be found. Henry, Tanya, and Philip opted to join them. Debbie followed me back to the bunk after we finished our coffee.

"Ally, wait up. I just wanted to say I am sorry. About earlier. I believe you, and anyway, it is none of my business. It's just that we are a small, isolated group living on top of each other," she laughed. "Literally. And it is easier, and sadly more entertaining, to believe the worst gossip. Can we forget it?"

"Sure, Debbie." I smiled. "Thank you. I feel like I can use

every ally I can muster." I told her the sordid details about my exchanges with Fedder.

"Ughh. Ally, I am so sorry. That is horrible. What are you going to do? I mean, are you going to tell someone or just avoid him?"

"I don't know. What should I say? He made an inappropriate pass at me? He didn't threaten me or promise me any quid pro quo if I slept with him. I am twenty-six, not sixteen. Will it do me more harm than good to report this? And maybe I did or said something that made him think I'd be game." And that, my friends, is how Gen X handled sexual harassment in the nineties. I still cringe when I remember this.

I could not fall asleep that night. I kept going over the Fedder situation in my head. Had I done something to encourage him? Was it the jean shorts or the dig gossip that I was trading my favors for dessert? Something Philip said? Regardless, I was mortified.

It reminded me of an incident several years earlier. I was barely twenty and was getting my hair cut at my mother's salon by a very cute, Israeli stylist. He cut my hair a few times and would always flirt with me while doing it. Occasionally, we would even step out for a smoke before, after, or during the session. He was in his mid-thirties and married with a couple of kids. I was too naive to recognize that this was perhaps not appropriate. Or maybe just too flattered to care. I assumed a little workplace back and forth for an hour every three to four months was harmless. My ego got the better of my good sense.

At any rate, the last time I was in his chair, he was going on about how the young girls working the desk wanted to fuck him. They kept telling him so. Then he leaned in, his mouth close enough to my face that I could feel his breath, and murmured,

"But not nearly as much as I want to fuck you."

I was stunned. Again, I could be vulgar with the best of them. But this was different. This man was fifteen years my senior, and the directness of his indecent proposal was shocking to me. So what did I do? Nothing. I said nothing. I sat in silence as he finished my hair, avoiding his eyes. When he was done, I nervously bolted for the reception area past my mom and out the door. And when she caught up with me, she looked at me and said, "Ally, weren't you wearing earrings when we got here?"

"No. No, I don't think so," I said, touching my ears.

"Yes. I am sure of it. The pearl and diamond drops the Katz's gave you for high school graduation. You must have left them at Elia's station. Run back in and grab them."

I looked at her then, square in the eye with the horror and humiliation of what just transpired all over my face and said, "Mom, please. I can't go back there. Please, can you just go in and grab them?"

My eyes pleaded my case, and it was as if she saw me, saw the whole thing, and understood. Maybe she had seen all of it over the last year and was just keeping her mouth shut. Whatever it was, she understood. Wordless, she pressed her red lips together and went back into the salon to Elia's chair where she grabbed my earrings. She said something to him. I have no idea what. She wasn't yelling. Her mouth was moving, and he was nodding. And then she came out. Pressing the earrings into my hand, her brown eyes met mine, and she said softly, "Here you go." And she held onto my hand for a bit as we walked uptown without speaking. It wasn't until we were alone in the elevator that she said quietly without looking at me, "Sweetheart, maybe you should find someone to cut your hair in Philly?"

We never said another word about it. Honestly, it was one of the few times in my life I felt my mother truly saw me and had my back. A part of me wished she could have said something like "It was not your fault, Ally. He is a grown man and should know better," or maybe "Sweetie, it's okay. This kind of thing happens to all of us." I wish she could have said anything that helped me not feel so ashamed or held a grown-up responsible for his actions. But again, these were not conversations we had in the nineties. It would be another twenty years before a woman was brave enough to tell her story and others said, "No more!" to the shame and echoed, "ME TOO!"

CHAPTER 11

A BIGGER TANGLE

The weekend could not come fast enough. The herd had thinned substantially by the time we left on Saturday. Aggie had mysteriously disappeared midweek, allegedly running season-related errands for Dicky, but I wondered if Turbo's fight with his wife had anything to do with it. Maybe Marilyn caught them in a compromising position, or at least she caught him trying, and Aggie was sent away or ducked out to avoid the drama. Dicky and Pano were off to Ephesus to discuss the translation of some engravings uncovered this season on both digs. Philip and Tanya were tagging along just to get the ride to Selcuk and planned to hit the beaches there. Turbo and Henry were staying behind, wrapping up dig business and playing host to Fedder and Gonzalez, who I had not even seen since the day he showed up. Those two would be gone by the time we got back and would not return until the donors' event. I cannot say I was disappointed. I just needed to avoid Todd Fedder until then.

The twenty-four hours preceding our departure were without incident. Turbo was constantly gushing over Fedder. I suspected he wanted to avoid anyone but himself being quoted in the magazine. Marilyn disappeared discreetly at some point on the last day. With neither her nor Aggie about, I guess Turbo had some time on his hands. At any rate, it kept Fedder out of my hair.

Finally, it was Saturday. I struggled to get through the workday. The promise of good food and a comfy bed was a merciless distraction.

After quick showers, we grabbed a bunch of tea biscuits and some cans of nectarine juice and started piling into the car.

We were about to get moving when Kat waved to us, calling out, “I’ll be right there! I just want to grab a drink!”

Six wide eyes shot to Kamal. He shrugged and mouthed, “Sorry, she had nothing else to do.”

Seconds later, she was squeezing past Simon for shotgun and plopping into the seat with a beer.

“Cheers. Right. Let’s get on.” Simon, Debbie, and I squeezed into the back. Me on the bump. And we were off.

I want to be sure not to overstate this. Kamal was the most terrifying driver ever. I might have felt a little security being held firmly in place by a body to both my left and right, but his car had no seat belts in the back. There was no speed limit being observed, and he passed everyone in front of him regardless of how many lanes were on the roadway. The better part of the drive was a single narrow lane in both directions hugging the sharp cliffs of Turkey’s west coast. We narrowly avoided no fewer than a dozen head-on collisions. There was no AC, and with the windows wide open, any sudden stop or impact would have ejected us all to our deaths.

That said, you can’t be mad at a guy who played a ninety-minute mixtape that included hits from U2, The Beastie Boys, Queen, The Cure, and many more legends of the eighties and nineties, and he sang every word at the top of his lungs. Which is probably why he couldn't hear me screaming.

As dusk fell, I could see Cesme in the distance and reasoned God was not so cruel as to let me glimpse paradise only to allow me to die moments later in a fiery crash. The water was a blood pressure–settling shade of turquoise. The descent from the cliffs to the village was breathtaking. The sky was exploding in purple and red as the setting sun inched closer to the water. The homes were arranged along neat, straight streets leading to the sea. There were both single and multi-family dwellings. Some were older or at least more traditional, most were plaster, and all were clean and well-maintained. The view from above was a patchwork of terracotta roofs. Mostly everyone had retired to their homes to get cleaned up and ready for dinner. The few women and girls still in the street at this time wore dresses, shorts, and tanks. Not a covered head in sight. We were less than a two-hour drive but yet a million miles away from Geyre.

I really couldn't shove a cigarette in my mouth fast enough when the car door opened. I heard Ayeleen calling out to Kamal. She was waving from a balcony three floors up and yelling something in Turkish to him. Kamal reported his parents were just finishing dinner and cocktails with a neighbor and heading back. Our dinner was all ready and casually laid out on the second-floor terrace facing the sea.

It was a gorgeous spread. Many of the things were similar fare to what was served to us at the dig, but what a difference when prepared by the loving hands of a mother missing her only son. In contrast, our meals at the site were the product of a pair of otherwise would-be farm hands who probably were counting the days until we all left them in peace and they could return to their day jobs.

Eggplant boats, fresh mezze, kofta, chicken kava,

homemade pita, Mediterranean salad, and cheeses all set on pretty, glazed ceramic serving dishes and garnished with home garden herbs. Plates, flatware, and cloth napkins were stacked to the side. Ayeleen jumped down the last couple of stairs laughing and pushed a bottle of wine at Kamal without looking at him and headed right for the food. Kamal and she had a very sibling exchange in Turkish, and then she said to nobody in particular in English, "Sorry. I am starving. Kamal reprimanded me for my rudeness, but really, I am dying. Anne, or Mom, said I was not to touch the food until Kamal and his friends arrived."

She winked at her brother who was opening the bottle. "Hello, Kat. It is nice to see you. What a surprise." She already had half a pita shoved in her mouth. "Simon, Debbie." She kissed them both, holding out her glass for Kamal to fill, and walked past us to sit at the table. "Well, I advise you all to sit and eat because I really could devour most of this myself." So we all joined her.

"Ayeleen, I thought Emel was coming," Kamal said.

"She will meet us at the beach tomorrow. Her *nine* (grandma) is here this week, so she is staying with her tonight," she answered through a full mouth. "Kamal used to be mad about her," she said, laughing, looking at Debbie and me. "Simon, Kamal tells me you're a Baba now! Congratulations. I want to see a photo, please. And Debbie, Kamal says you are engaged! Congratulations, as well. And I hear Tanya and Phil are well... you know. Holy shit. I don't see you guys for a few weeks, and wow. Ally, how are you keeping score for your first summer here?" She pinched my arm.

Everyone was laughing and chatting. I liked Ayeleen when I met her at Ephesus, but didn't fully appreciate how bubbly she was. So confident and funny. So different from Akara. They came from different worlds. They were the same nationality, same religion, age, spoke the same language, and even came from the same region, but I had more in common with Ayeleen.

Kamal's family wasn't wealthy on the scale of the donors coming from Istanbul, but they were comfortable and privileged compared to the rural peasant farmers who populated the village near the site. Their world was secular. Their children, including the girls, were educated and had opportunities for careers. While it is true the girls and women of Geyre and villages like it all over Turkey in 1998 had none of the above, it is not like the boys and men of those villages had much in the way of options. Still, I couldn't help but feel very sorry for Deniz's sister. Ayeleen would have to be brave, but there was a path forward for her, even more so if she could get settled in the US. I was not an idiot regarding the way of things outside of my Western world. This was just the first time I ever really experienced it, so to speak. It also occurred to me that she may have serious reservations about leaving. Most likely, she loved Turkey and her life here and would be really devastated to leave. I am embarrassed to admit, up to that point, I think I only ever voted once in my life, in 1996. I had taken everything for granted. My sense of entitlement was a little sickening, even to me.

We stayed up drinking and talking until late. Kamal's parents eventually came back, kissing everyone and shuffling off to bed.

When we came down the next morning, a typical Turkish breakfast of cheese, bread, tomatoes, cured meats, and nectarines plucked from the tree in the small garden was already laid out. His anne was steaming milk for the coffee, and his baba was on a ladder in the garden talking to his fig and olive trees.

"Herkese Gunaydin! Sorry, good morning, everyone. Coffee is on table and milk coming. So nice to see you all again. Hello, my dear, you must be Ali. We did not meet properly last night."

"Yes, thank you so much for having me. Is there anything I can do to help?"

"Ally, please don't embarrass us all by being useful. It raises the bar." Ayeleen winked.

"Cheeky!" Their anne playfully rapped her daughter on the head with a dish towel. "No, thank you, my dear. Enjoy." She was cutting up a melon now and putting it in a cooler with cans of apricot juice and bottles of water. "I am leaving for you to take to the beach. Ayeleen will carry it." She raised a brow at her daughter. She disappeared after kissing Kamal on the head. Ayeleen rolled her eyes.

"So wha time shu we 'ead out?" Simon asked, humming while he cleaned his plate. "I could be sor'ed in firty minutes o so?"

We all agreed and met by the kitchen with towels, sunscreen, etc. in hand. Ayeleen had the small cooler, Kamal grabbed an umbrella from the alley path leading to the garden, and we were off.

"So, Kamal, are we going to that great little place for lunch? The place we went last year?"

"No, Debbie," Ayeleen chimed in. "My friend Emel and I have been eating our way through town all summer. We have a better place near the nude beach. She is coming, too. We thought about a late lunch because we got up so late, and we found the best place for ice cream." Kat made a face. "What, you don't like Turkish ice cream, Kat?"

"I suppose it is one acquired taste I never acquired," said

Kat, flipping her bob. Everyone was laughing.

"I am sorry, what am I missing? It's ice cream. And I would assume it's like gelato, no?" I asked.

"Not quite, Ally. It is kind of...well...chewy." Debbie was scrunching her nose and giggling.

"What do you mean chewy?"

"You'll see," Kat added haughtily.

The sky was at least three perfect shades of blue and clear save a whisper of thin clouds. We walked several blocks away from the beach closest to the house in order to be closer to our lunch destination. A pleasant breeze blew off the Aegean and brought with it a whiff of lavender and hibiscus. I inhaled deeply, and my mind wandered to thoughts of an ancient world here untamed and unspoiled. I was daydreaming and not processing the scene we were slowly approaching. A man was turning a drum that looked like a cotton candy machine and spinning a taffy-like substance onto a cone he handed to a young woman who stood with another woman in front of him. Yikes. That must be the chewy ice cream.

The women walked away holding hands and licking the cone simultaneously. Their ice cream–coated lips lingered in a deep kiss. They pulled away laughing, holding each other's gaze. My group slowed to a stop. We stood face to face with Turbo's wife, Marilyn, and a beet-red Aggie, still holding hands.

We all stood looking stunned, facing one another on the boardwalk. All of us except Kat. She smiled from ear to ear.

"Well, well," she purred, "fancy meeting you two here. Together."

"I, ugh, Kat..." Aggie sputtered in a panic. But Marilyn was as cool as a cucumber. "Hello, Kat. Lovely to see you again. All going well this season? Rob did say how vital your work has been to his book. In fact, he mentioned you were looking to make the move across the Pond in the near future."

Kat didn't miss a beat. "Yes. That was my plan. Alas, Dicky is convinced the best use of my talents lies at Oxford."

"Nonsense. I am certain Rob finds you invaluable to his current work and necessary in NYC. Aggie here is more than capable of sorting Dicky on her own at Oxford. I am confident Rob can and will convince him otherwise. Leave it to me. Looks like we'll be ships that cross in the night though." She sighed, her lips curling up a bit. "It seems my research will keep me abroad more in the future."

"Is that so?" Kat's eyes were locked on Aggie. "Well then. Let's hope for all our sakes it works out. Would you like to join us for lunch? Or are you... otherwise engaged?"

Aggie steeled herself. "No, we won't. But thank you so much. We already have plans." She smiled at Marilyn.

"Well then. Ta!" And with that, Kat walked one way, and Aggie and Marilyn the other. We all just stood for a second dumbly before we caught up with Kat. They were well out of earshot before anyone said a word. It was Kamal who spoke first.

"What the fuck?!"

"I cunna may meself bileeve eit!" Simon added. "Aggay an Merrilyn? Theys a turna!" Debbie shot me a look that said "Huh?" and then turned on Kat.

"Kat, did you basically suggest you'd expose them to Turbo if Marilyn didn't help get you a place at NYU? Presumably working with, or should I say under, Turbo?"

"Debbie, stop clutching your pearls and grow up. These guys play us to suit their needs all the bloody time, and what is in it for us? I'll keep my mouth shut and come to NYU. I'll help that lecherous prick finish his bleedin' book, and then I'm out. I want to get a job at a tech startup. Maybe stay in the States and make some money in my lifetime. I don't give a shit about Turbo. For all I know, he already knows about this thing with his wife and Aggie. He probably cares more that Aggie wanted her and not him, egomaniacal bastard. And I know for sure he does not want the academic community wasting breath whispering about this nonsense instead of blowing sunshine up his ass about the fuckin' most boring book published ever. And a divorce wouldn't help Marilyn any, as I happen to know that Rob has a ton of family money, and they have a prenup. So, yes, Debbie. That is exactly what I was suggesting."

"So, what is your plan? To jump off the plane and into Rob's bed until you find a better offer? That seems opportunistic."

"Don't judge me, Debbie. I'm not some doe-eyed babe in the woods. I know what Turbo is, and I don't want anything from him except to get to New York and the hell away from Dicky in the bargain."

"You mean Dicky tried to get in your pants too?" Debbie looked stricken. She was literally clutching her necklace now.

"No. Dicky keeps his hands off my ass. He is just a lazy, drunken sod who wants to keep me under his thumb to do all the work, including the last three papers he published. If I'm going to get fucked, I want to at least get off." And with that, Kat stormed onto the sand, spread out her towel, and flopped onto her back.

We stood still for a moment, eyes wide and mouths agape. Then Simon shrugged his shoulders and headed onto the sand to join Kat. The rest of us just followed in silence.

"What is a tech startup?" I mouthed to Kamal.

"That was your takeaway from that shit show?" He burst

out laughing. “Ally, I might be in love with you!” He whispered quietly in my ear. But maybe not quietly enough because I caught Debbie’s eye as he leaned in and saw her frown. Shit. This day was getting gooier than the damn ice cream.

We spent the rest of the morning and early afternoon in strained silence, but by lunch, it was like a weight had been lifted. The color of the water, the sweetness of the breeze, really, you would have to have witnessed a puppy massacre to stay in a solemn mood. And what really was at stake here? Turbo had been carrying on for God knows how long and with whom. Who knows what kind of threats or promises he had made in that time to get what he wanted? Based on what Aggie had told me, he was pretty aggressive. Kat could take care of herself. Anyway, with his attention span, he’d probably be reaching for an undergrad before Kat was over the jet lag. And Marilyn staying married to him despite her preferences at least forced some degree of discretion from him, which probably saved his career. So if Kat somehow benefited and saw this as her ticket out from under Dicky, who had been unjustly taking advantage of her for years, who cared? I didn’t see any innocents here. Even Aggie was complicit in the adultery. I was just a little amazed at how easy it seemed for all of them to stretch the lines that tethered them to morality and get all tangled up in the process.

The restaurant Ayeleen and her friend chose did not disappoint. Emel met us there at one-thirty, a bottle of white wine already on ice next to our table. There were Turkish greetings and introductions and a nod to the waiter as we all took our seats.

“I took the liberty of ordering. Everything is good here. I hope it was not... presumptuous? Is that the word?” Emel drawled, pushing a lock of salon-blown, dark, dirty blond hair behind her ear. Plates of fresh seafood and grilled vegetables were laid out.

"Not a' all luv. Gorgeous this," Simon gushed appreciatively, helping himself. Emel shot Ayeleen a confused look, to which she responded with a shrug. We all dug in, oohing and umming our approval. Emel ate nothing but instead lit a cigarette and sipped at her wine. I liked her instantly.

Two bottles of wine later, we all sat back in our chairs, sleepy and satisfied.

"So, Emel, what is your plan after the summer?" Kamal asked her from the other side of the table.

"Ayeleen did not say? I will be moving to London. My brother and his wife are there. I'll be working with him. For the business."

"Emel's family owns a company that exports Turkish specialty foods worldwide," Ayeleen explained to the group. "That's why I asked her to order for us. She is a pro." Ayeleen winked at her friend.

"That's exciting," Debbie chimed in. "Well, your English is perfect."

"Yes. It was either London behind a desk or Istanbul under some olive merchant. Family duty. Fuck that." She waved a manicured hand and pulled deeply on her smoke. I really liked her.

"On that note, shall we?" Kat was on her feet and halfway toward the exit before the rest of us followed suit.

"Emel's parents will be attending the donors' event at the dig," Ayeleen mentioned as we all headed back to our beach set up.

"Fancy," teased Kamal, and Emel rolled her eyes.

"Actually, circumstances have overtaken them. They will be

sending friends as surrogates. My father was very disappointed to hear of your... nuptials, Kamal," she teased back. "Not that you were a particularly desirable prospect; you were at least a decent last resort." Kamal put both of his hands over his heart and feigned a wounded expression. Emel rolled her hazel eyes and turned toward me.

"Ali, you are an architect in New York, yes?"

"Yes, well I will be. Once I have a job."

"My father's sister is bringing Abraham Nifoussi to the reception. He is a dear friend and will be visiting. You should introduce yourself. I will tell him he needs to know you."

Abraham Nifoussi was a named partner at a "hot" practice in The City. His firm was on the list Eve gave me.

"Thank you. I really appreciate it, Emel. You don't even know me...."

"I know all I need to know," she said, winking at Kamal. "Now I must go. Ayeleen." And with that, she kissed Ayeleen on both cheeks, gave us all a ciao, and got into a car I didn't even notice was waiting for her. Debbie was looking at me with a tight mouth.

"Who do I owe for lunch?" she finally said. "Think I was in the bathroom when the bill came."

We all realized none of us had paid the bill.

"We have to go back! Oh my God." I was panicking. Kamal and Ayeleen were smiling knowingly at each other.

"I am sure there was no bill." Said Ayeleen. "Emel's family owns half this town."

Back on the beach, I donned my huge glasses and hat and tuned everyone out. I needed a minute to take stock of the last few hours. So, Turbo was a gross creep trying to move on Aggie. However, whether he was aware of it or not, Aggie was already sleeping with his wife. And while it had been clear throughout the season that Kat was trying to get Turbo's attention, it was solely for the purpose of sleeping her way across the pond where she would jump ship as soon as a better opportunity presented itself. Now it seemed Turbo's wife would be Kat's ally in getting out from under Dicky figuratively and under Turbo, literally, so that she could carry on with Aggie. Meanwhile, Kamal and Ayeleen had a very well-connected friend who may or may not help me network for a job in NYC. I may have been reading the body language wrong, but was it possible Kamal said something to her to encourage her generosity? I think Debbie sure thought so. I did not appreciate whatever I was assuming she was assuming...wait, what? Again, stickier than the ice cream.

Nobody mentioned Aggie and Marilyn Turbo the whole drive home. Maybe we were just tired or wanted to pretend to know nothing about it. Or maybe it was Kamal's open windows and loud music, but I was grateful. Anyway, it seemed the women were ruthlessly pulling the strings here and for better or worse, it made for a nice change.

We pulled into the gravel drive of the site around nine p.m. We all muttered our goodnights and scuffled off to our respective bunks. Debbie and I did not exchange a word until we were washed, brushed, and tucked into our cots. I was just dozing off when she perked up.

"I can't believe about Aggie and Marilyn! You know what I mean?" she spewed. "All of that time Turbo was trying to corner her and like there was no way! Do you think he knows? And that Kat. Can you believe her? Trying to take advantage of that mess for her own benefit. She's got a nerve. You know what I mean?"

"No, Debbie. I'm not sure I do know what you mean. Dicky has been taking advantage of her in a non-physical way since she apparently was an undergrad, taking credit for her work. If she is playing the situation to her benefit now, I can't say it's admirable, but really, I don't blame her. Anyway, it really isn't our business."

"Well. I guess I shouldn't be surprised you'd say that."

"Excuse me?"

"Nothing. Never mind. Goodnight." She sighed deeply and I heard her turn over. She was quiet for a minute and then half shouted, "Ally, please. I know you are fooling around with Kamal! It is so obvious. Shame on you. He is married...."

"Wait, what? What the hell are you talking about?"

"I see the looks he gives you...the whispers. Getting his rich friend to hook you up in New York. What do you care if he gets deported?"

"What the hell are you talking about? I thought we already litigated this. We are friends. That's all. If his family friend offered to help me with an introduction, it was just out of kindness, Debbie. And really, I don't think I have to justify myself to you. I am just minding my own business, but you are ALL CRAZY!"

"I don't know, Ally. There seems to be a lot of smoke around you. Deniz, Kamal, and now alleged Fedder nonsense. And you always seem to have a story to either explain it away or make you the victim. Where there's smoke there's fire, Ally. Maybe Philip is right, and you just chew people up and spit them out."

That was enough, not to mention unjustified. I was seething but really too tired, too disgusted to go head-to-head with her. I just looked her way in the dim moonlight through our windows and said "FUCK. YOU. DEBBIE" and turned away from her. Tears burned my eyes, but I would not let her hear so much as a sniffle.

I was standing on quicksand. In an effort to keep quiet my scheme to help Deniz's sister, I had left myself open to some nasty assumptions. Additionally, it was clear that people were assuming there was more there than just friendship between me and Kamal. Was he just flirting or was he serious? Regardless, even though I was never going to act on that, we both really needed to be careful. One word from the wrong person, and he could find himself in real trouble. And Fedder? That creep was completely out of line. *No way* I was taking any heat for *that.*

My exhaustion won out over my outrage that night, and I did get to sleep. But it was fitful and full of disturbing dreams.

I was on the beach out in Quogue. My happy place. I was sprawled on a towel and could feel the warmth of the sun on my skin like a hug, its rays energizing me and filling me with love and strength. A steady breeze kept me cool. The gently breaking waves were a soothing mantra. I breathed deeply and was at peace. Then the wind changed and brought with it a feeling of dread. I sat up on my elbows to see the sky and ocean darken. The steady rhythmic surf became a rising tsunami that towered over me as I stood now looking up at a black wall of water. Every instinct screamed to me "Run!" but I could not. My legs were like columns of stone. I barely managed to back up a bit, and when I did, I felt my body against a wall, or was it a dune or a person or just a force? It did not matter because now I was filled with terror in the shadow of the tidal wave cresting over my head, and I could feel it pulling me under before the water smothered me. Like a rip current, but I was still on dry land and it was pulling me down, down into the wall of water. Just before everything went black, I heard muffled cries, like someone yelling my name underwater. "Allughh, Akurr!!!"

I woke drenched in sweat. It took me a moment to realize

where I was. A speaker bleated "Allahu Akbar, Allahu Akbar!" The first call to prayer. I exhaled deeply remembering the shit show from the previous day. Well, I wasn't exactly safe, but at least I was on dry land.

It was Monday, and the donors were coming on Friday. Five days. In that time, I had to wrap up my inking and avoid triggering a land mine. Things with Debbie were tense to say the least.

We barely spoke. Truly, I did not have to try too hard to avoid her. Meals were less formal now as everyone was scrambling to finish their seasonal assignments. Food was laid out more buffet style, and we could drop in, grab, and go or sit if we had time.

Kamal and I presented Akara with a pile of books; he actually drove over to Geyre. We met Deniz there, and he helped Kamal unload them and stash them in the storage area that I think belonged to the restaurant that employed our dig's kitchen staff. He could bring them home a few at a time without raising suspicions and swap them out for new ones as she finished them. Of course, Philip and Tanya spied me in Geyre walking with Deniz to where Kamal was parked to get another armful of books. I did not acknowledge them. At this point, I gave zero fucks.

We met her one last time to say goodbye, and she was very overcome. Deniz told her who provided the books, and she finally looked right at Kamal with a smile of pure joy in her eyes.

She held onto his hands and thanked him and blessed him. Tears were in both of their eyes. He just nodded and said something quietly to her in Turkish that made her smile and nod back. Then she left with Deniz.

I don't know what ever became of her. I don't know if she

was found out and punished, or if she ever even read those books. Maybe she devoured them all, insisted on going further, and defied expectations, blazing a trail for women and girls in her village and others like it. I will never know. I do know that in that moment, I was proud of us all. I admired Akara's curiosity and drive, I was touched by her brother's desire to risk his own neck for his sister, and I loved Kamal a little for being complicit with me. Whether it was out of the kindness of his heart or just to impress me, he didn't need to get involved, yet he did. And yes. I felt good about trying to help another young woman stand strong on her own two feet, regardless of the fact that I felt unsteady myself.

CHAPTER 12

THE EVENT

The evening of the donor party finally arrived. Technically, we were guests, but until the first "official" guests arrived, we were instructed to help set up and close out the site for the season. The next morning, I would catch the shit bus to Izmir airport, take a quick flight from Izmir to Istanbul, and then back to New York. Henry, Philip, and Tanya were all stopping in Istanbul for a few days. The four of us would be traveling that far together. Tension with Philip was at a breaking point, but I only had to make it one more day. It would be a shame if we couldn't just part as friends, but I would settle for not having a blow-out.

Marilyn resurfaced on site late last night, bringing Fedder and Gonzalez in her wake. Nobody had seen any of them yet. According to Henry, the press had gathered plenty of material already, and tonight was really about shots of the event and a few quotes from the socialites.

After breakfast, I put the final touches on my ink drawings. Henry was in the studio, packing and straightening up. He would be returning to Aphrodisias to officially close out the season after his jaunt to Istanbul. He surveyed my sheets and smiled.

"Well, you pulled it off, Ally. Not going to lie, I was a little worried at the beginning. Especially when Philip mentioned you were a lefty."

"He what?" I was visibly annoyed.

"Yeah, well, I don't think he meant anything by it. He was just, well, he just mentioned you were a lefty." Didn't mean anything by it my ass.

"Henry, we both know Philip has been doing his best to get in my way since I got here. I am done apologizing and explaining. It's true, I'm an imperfect human being, but I have done nothing to warrant his vitriol. And it is also true that I'm a lefty, yet I managed somehow to draw rocks in plan and elevation. I do have a fucking master's degree from Penn, for God's sake!" I was standing now and kind of screaming in his face. To his credit, he did not seem ruffled.

"Okay, okay. Really, I am not trying to start anything. You know as well as anybody drafting lefty is more challenging. I am sorry I doubted you, but you know I have skin in the game with this book." He held his hands up and stepped toward me, smiling. "And Philip has been a prick. You shouldn't let it get to you. I thought he was a prick last year, and he will probably be one next year." He was right in front of me. "You okay?"

I calmed down. Henry was one of the few really genuine people I met here. He was an ally in the drama. He was a friend. "Yeah. Yeah, I'm fine, Henry. Just a little pre-travel jitters. And I am worried about what is waiting for me at home. My family has a lot of expectations. I am not sure I can deliver. Sorry. I didn't mean to shout at you."

"We should get together when you are back in the city. I want to hear all about the new job, when you have one. You can bitch about how hard you are working, and I can complain about university politics to a civilian."

"I would love that, Henry. Thank you." He gave me a solid hug, which I really needed.

Unfortunately, Philip walked into the studio at that exact moment, muttering, "For fuck's sake." I stalked out without even acknowledging him, smiling with my head held high.

After lunch, I walked with Pano to the museum to get our assignments and found Dicky in a tizzy. He was shouting at a short, dark man and swigging a canteen filled with something I doubted was water.

"Bloody hell, man. What are you saying?"

"Pardon me, Dicky," Pano diplomatically interrupted, "Can I help?"

"I bloody well hope so. There is some issue with this evening. I can't get the bottom of it. This man is very difficult, and I dare say he doesn't understand a word of English." Dicky was sweating profusely.

The man rolled his eyes behind Dicky's back. Clearly, his grasp of English was not so tenuous. Pano smiled at him and pulled him to the side so that Dicky could not hear their conversation. In English. When he returned, he reported the bottom line.

"This gentleman is the event coordinator. His name is Omer. There is a little snag. They had planned on using two food trucks pulled right up to the back of the museum to stage the food as close as possible. One is having equipment issues and cannot be used. No panic though, he has staked out the kitchen and says they can regroup and set up there. But given the distance, they will need some extra hands. He wanted to know if he could ask the dig kitchen staff to step up and serve. He will cover it."

Dicky looked startled. "Right. Well. Tell him to get on then! I think I saw those fellows about." He was looking around like they might be hiding behind a sarcophagus.

Pano smiled at Omer. "Let me take you to the kitchen. Deniz and Mirac should be there. Hopefully they have no other plans."

They walked off toward the kitchen, and I turned to follow, not wanting to be left alone with Dicky.

"Ally, maybe you could put in a good word. Seeing how chummy you are with that lot!" Dicky called after us. And the bastard winked at me! Son of a bitch. I reddened and stalked off.

We gathered in front of the museum at six-thirty p.m. The tension in the air was ripe. I felt like I was in a sweaty version of a daytime soap with a less attractive, surlier cast. Debbie's eyes shifted regularly to the drive waiting for her fiancé to arrive. He was duc earlier that day but was apparently delayed. Simon was staring down the caterer's truck, trying to scent dinner. Kat stood next to Turbo, eying Aggie with the slightest hint of a smirk as Marilyn casually breezed across the drive and took a place on his other side. Fedder and Gonzalez walked through the party set up, the former leering in my direction every so often as thc latter checked the composition for various shots. Pano stood a few feet off between Dicky and the event coordinator Omer, acting as the English-to-English translator and referee. Dicky's shirt was rumpled and half-tucked, and he was already swinging a drink. Henry was oddly nowhere to be found.

Turbo prattled on about the importance of this evening to the site and the university and our contribution to architectural history and academia, blah blah. I was so focused on tuning him out while trying to calculate all of the ways this could go south, I didn't even notice Kamal sidle up close and whisper, "You look nice" in my ear. Tanya and Phil stood practically shoulder to shoulder, grinning smugly.

I was wearing the flowy Turkish cotton lace sun dress I bought in Selcuk and, for better or worse, my infamous gladiator sandals. I did the math and determined I could navigate the museum floor without killing myself. My skin was deeply tanned by this point and, shy of a little lip gloss, needed no makeup. My hair was pulled back in a sleek, dark ponytail. I looked natural. I looked native. I looked pretty, if I do say so myself, and Kamal noticed. So what?

The guests were due at seven for cocktails and "heavy hors d'oeuvres." There was a table set up with cold mezze, olives, cheeses, etc. Deniz and Mirac were passing around hot apps and collecting dirty glasses. There was a three-piece group playing traditional Turkish music. This was meant to be a very civilized, understated event to thank the donors and drum up some more cash. Turbo would give a brief thank-you speech mentioning what was "new" on site. He would, of course, mention his book as well as the *Life Magazine* article as proof of continued interest.

Donors would also be getting a plaque listing their names in the foyer of the Upper East Side Institute for the Study of the Ancient World or "The Institute." This was not a gala. Just cocktails. Assuming everyone could stay sober enough to hold it together for two-plus hours, what could go wrong? Oy.

In addition to the donors, a few of the higher-ups from Ephesus were expected. This probably explained why Dicky was tweaking. Gerta always unraveled him. Also, it was likely well known in the academic community that Dicky was a useless drunk and Turbo was a... self-promoting adolescent who couldn't keep his dick in his pants. The pair of them might need a little babysitting to keep this thing from blowing up.

The group broke like billiard balls as soon as Turbo ended his spiel. He took a half step toward Aggie but was immediately redirected by Marilyn to Dicky, who was now waving two drinks. I made for the shade and shoved a cigarette in my mouth. Henry lit it before I saw him.

"Hey, where have you been?"

"Making sure all of the drawings are in order. Nice work again, Southpaw. Like I said, you pulled it off." He lit himself one.

I smiled gratefully. "Sorry again about earlier. You were right. Ink is not my forte. I am glad I did a decent job of it."

"Anyway, chances are you will never see ink and Mylar again. Everything is done by CAD now."

"Well then I'm fucked because I can't do that either."

"What do they teach you at Penn these days?"

"Mainly humiliation and self-loathing."

"Ahh. Right. Can I buy you a drink before we have to play hosts?"

"Sure. Henry, I want to thank you for your help this summer. You know, navigating the ins and outs. And for being so... neutral. This place was such a minefield. I wasn't expecting so much, well, drama, I guess. And pettiness."

"Are you kidding? Academics are the worst. Bored, unfulfilled, and cynical. And very ungrateful for the opportunity they are given to peer at human history so close up."

"Henry, I didn't know you were also a philosopher," I teased.

"It was my minor." He winked and hooked his arm through

mine. "You better hold on tight. I see you have those stupid shoes on again."

Deniz was circulating throughout the crew with a tray of raki in tall thin glasses. Henry and I grabbed two and toasted. Kamal sauntered over with a beer as the first car pulled up.

"Ah, let the games begin," Henry rushed to the slowing Rolls-Royce to welcome the first of our guests, leaving us alone. I spied Debbie with Andrik, finally, smiling psychotically and drinking the raki.

"So, all packed?" Kamal whispered as he leaned in casually.

"Just about. You?"

"I brought most of my stuff back last weekend. I'll be back there for another week before I have to get back to... back to school." His face was too close to my ear. Those impossible lashes. I swear I could feel them tickle my face, my ears, neck... And he smelled like honey.

"And... and Ayeleen?" I coughed, raki almost coming out my nose.

He chuckled. "She will travel with me. I need to get her settled before classes start. Ah, look, another sucker arrives." He nodded toward the stretch Benz rolling up to the museum. A tall, very tan man with dark glasses stepped out of the car. He looked over his shades at an elegant woman being helped out of the other side.

"That, Ally, is Abraham Nifoussi. Let me introduce you. I have met him a few times. My parents were engineers on an Izmir residential building he designed a few years back."

"He has quite a presence. Who is that woman? His wife?"

"No. That is Emel's Aunt. He isn't married. He is... I think he prefers..."

"I get it." The nineties were still a little repressed. "Please introduce me."

He put his hand on my back and led me toward the arriving cars. Nifoussi recognized Kamal as we approached and shook his hand, saying something in Turkish to him.

"Mr. Nifoussi, this is my friend Ally. She is an architect in New York."

"Yes, yes of course, Miss Acker, Emel's friend. Charmed to meet you, my dear." He gallantly kissed my hand.

"Mr. Nifoussi, I am a huge fan of your work. I did my graduate thesis on adaptive reuse of forgotten construction along the west side of Manhattan and proposed threading the sites together to create an elevated public space. Your book, *The Elegance and Poetry of the Urban Ruin,* inspired me." I was blushing and gushing and making an ass of myself.

"Ally, my dear, you are welcome to visit me in The City and tell me how wonderful I am. Tonight, I am simply arm candy. Walk with me and tell me what is new at ancient Aphrodisias." He put his hand on my elbow. "Ally, this is my dear friend, Ela Mizrahi."

The elegant woman stepped around the car. She was wearing a huge Hermès scarf tied into a halter dress and at her hips was a three-tier chain Chanel belt. Purple jade earrings dangled from her ears, and a diamond ring that could sink the Titanic sat casually on her finger. Her eyebrows raised in my direction over huge sunglasses.

"Ally? Ally Acker? Darling! Come here! I know your mother!" I totally forgot about the Mizrahis. Rich Turkish Jews. This was Emel's father's sister? What a small world! She was in my mom's gallery group, and they were involved in some of the same charitable crap out at the Hamptons. She was the one my mother called to get the consulate engaged in my earthquake rescue. She grabbed me by the shoulders and kissed both cheeks.

"My dear, you look wonderful. Your mother has been so worried. Show us where the bar is, and we will be forever in your debt." I caught a glimpse of Kamal smiling and shaking his head as they dragged me off, one on each arm. I also saw the disapproving look on Philip's face, damn asshole. I didn't care one bit what he thought anymore.

As I guided them to the bar, Fedder popped out of nowhere and blocked our path.

"Toad, it's Toad, yes?" Mizrahi addressed Fedder dismissively. "The *Post* sent you all the way here to shoot this? I thought snapping pics of drunk heiresses getting out of cars in East Hampton without their knickers was more your level."

"Actually, I am writing an article for *Life* and would love a picture and a quote, Ela. And it is Todd." He smirked.

"I would be happy to pose for a picture with my friends, if they consent, and it is Mrs. Mizrahi," she returned coolly. "Make sure you get the caption correct. I am sure you are familiar with Abraham Nifoussi, and this is our dear friend, Ally Acker. She is the next new face to take New York's design scene by storm. She is fabulous."

"Yes, we have met, and I agree, she—"

"Just keep it in your pants and take the fucking picture, Toad. Smiling this long hurts my face and gives me wrinkles," she snapped back. The camera clicked and Gonzalez walked away. Mrs. Mizrahi and Mr. Nifoussi steered me past a slack-faced Fedder and toward the bar. Well played, Mrs. Mizrahi.

I chatted with her while Nifoussi ordered their martinis. Henry and Gerta walked an elderly couple through the gallery.

We were not an hour in when it was clear that Dicky was

drunk. Good and drunk. Kamal and I rushed to keep him from chatting up the donors too much and blowing the whole night. He was making an ass of himself in a group with Henry and Gerta. He dropped his drink and soaked the open-toed shoes of one of the grand dames. I grabbed him and found Aggie and asked her to babysit while Kamal tried to find Deniz or other staff to clean up his mess. I reminded her of how inconvenient it would be if Dicky was suspended.

From across the party, Kamal was swiftly making his way toward me, panic on his face. "Where is Deniz? I haven't seen him in like a half hour. The last I saw, he was bringing another round to Abe Nifoussi."

"Maybe he is in the kitchen?"

"Here, let's grab some of these glasses on our way. It's getting a little messy out here." We each filled a tray and hurried toward the kitchen in search of Deniz. Poor Mirac was maniacally jumping from group to group. Trying to serve, clean up, etc.

I caught Philip eyeing us. When was this guy not looking at me for God's sake? The kitchen was dark and quiet, which was weird. One of the caterer's crew should have been in here cleaning the dirties as Deniz and Mirac brought them back. Was Deniz attacked and carried off? We heard shuffling and a groan from the pantry. We looked at each other, then raced over, throwing open the door and smacking on the lights.

Deniz was shirtless and pressed against the counter under a young man who must have been from the caterer's crew. When the light went on, there was a lot of shouting and cursing in Turkish. Kamal had his hands up like a shield over his eyes and was backing away, repeating "Ozur dilerim, ozur dilerim." I too backed up, only to bump into Philip, who apparently followed us into the kitchen.

"Well, well, Ally. You couldn't resist, could you? I knew you were fucking him." It was then he spotted Deniz and the caterer's busboy, Adem, untangling themselves and putting their shirts on. "Uhh, well. Uhh." He stammered.

"Yeah, Phil. Uhh, well! What the hell are you doing following me and looking at me all the time? Mind your own fucking business!"

"I saw you two walking with trays toward the kitchen and figured it was an excuse to get some privacy. I guess I was wrong. About you and Deniz, too, apparently." Deniz and Adem stood there with terrified expressions on their faces. "Well, what the hell was I supposed to think, Ally?"

"I don't give a shit what you think, Philip. It is not for you to think about what the hell I do at all. It is not for you to care, to judge, to discuss. And you will keep your mouth shut about these two as well," I gestured toward the very embarrassed pair behind me, "because that is also none of your fucking business. Your fat mouth could get them fired, or worse for all we know. So get the hell out of here and get a fucking life!" I turned back to the pantry and barked, red-faced and breathless. "And as for you two, get dressed, get control of yourselves, and get back to work!"

I stormed past them all and out the kitchen door. The sun was getting low, and night was cooling off. I took a deep breath and closed my eyes. When I opened them, I saw Abe Nifoussi leaning against a sarcophagus, lighting two cigarettes in his mouth. He gestured for me to take one, so I walked over to him and did. He took a long drag, and when he exhaled, he drawled, "Well played, my dear. Very well played." He took another drag and grabbed my arm. "I like you. Come see me back in New

York."

We walked back to the party. An able-bodied group was assembling impromptu to watch the sunset from the theater. I saw Philip watching us and scowled at him. He had the sense to look away.

"Shall we join them?" Abe looked at Kamal and me.

It was still somewhat light out. And even after the sunset, the path was reasonably lit. But I thought of the time-worn stone stairs and the soles of my shoes. I shot Kamal a look of panic. He was already on the same page, looking at my feet.

"Abe, I'll take a walk with you. I am not sure about Ally's shoes..."

"Nonsense. We will escort her safely."

This had to be quick. It was already almost eight. The sun would set, we would walk back, Turbo would thank the donors, and this night would be over. Somehow, when I put it in that context, there did not seem to be time for the additional drama of me breaking my neck. So, off we went.

Turbo was already lecturing about the theater's history and use when we joined the group. I closed my ears to his voice and concentrated only on the faint sounds of music still coming from the reception. The sky was an explosion of pinks, oranges, and purples. The sweet sounds were gently amplified by the onset of darkness. Suddenly, shouting broke my trance.

It was Debbie, and she was shouting and sobbing from the direction of the museum. My instinct was to run to her, even after our fight, but I took two quick steps down the stairs at the theater and instantly slipped. Kamal and Abe caught me by the armpits.

"Ah, tragic death by fashion averted." I loved Abe.

Once I had two feet on the gravel path, Kamal and I hightailed it toward the yelling.

Debbie was in front of the museum, hysterically crying and throwing glasses at Andrik. Kamal and I stopped short of the scene that was very indiscreetly unfolding in front of the guests who did not attend the sunset but were getting a special show regardless.

"You asshole. Why did you ask me to marry you if you were still in love with her?"

"I didn't know. I didn't realize. She just showed up in Symi, and we just still worked. I'm sorry. It's just not over."

"And this was the best time to tell me? At a party with my colleagues? Did you think I wouldn't make a scene? You are a class-A asshole."

"I needed to tell you before tomorrow. I am meeting her in Santorini."

"Well, you can get going now!" She shrieked as she stalked away toward the bunk.

The guests were silent. Everyone was exchanging looks. Maybe they hadn't all heard or understood? Turbo was just leading the rest of the crowd back toward the courtyard. He walked with Gerta, resting his hand in the small of her back. He saw me and said, "Good, Ally, there you are. Have you seen Dicky? We are about to make the presentation and thank our guests for coming."

Mizrahi, standing nearby, caught my eye with a smirk and squeezed Turbo's arm. "Darling Robert, you always throw such an eventful reception."

He gave her a confused smile and grabbed a mic, quieting and gathering the guests. Dicky was eying him from a dark corner and was making his way through the crowd. His expression was determined and not a little unnerving.

Turbo started, "Good evening, ladies and gentlemen. It is always such a pleasure and an honor to host those whose continued interest and support make our work here possible year after year. This research, which we are privileged to conduct, honors your rich history and—"

"You bloody wanker bastard!" Oh. My. God. Dicky was pushing his way through the assembly toward Rob. He was drunk, and he was pissed, and he was out of control.

"I...I'm sorry, Dicky...perhaps..." His eyes shifted like a mad over the crowd, looking for help. He locked eyes with Kat, and her mouth just curved up in an amused grin.

"You pompous twat!" Dicky wasn't stopping. "You can't keep your dick in your pants, can you?" Oh, my God, this was happening! In front of everyone.

"First you try it on with Kat, then you try to nick Aggie out from under me to be your plaything in New York. To have her there with you in New York. Now you're trying to shag Gerta. Gerta, my one true love. What just to spite me? Well, I say I'm not having it! I've got all the pull with the boys up at Oxford, and I am telling you now, I don't care who you diddle, you're not takin' Aggie! She goes, then I go! Shut this whole bleeding pile of shit down for all I care." And with that, he bowed to the crowd. "Mesdames et Messieurs, merci et bonne nuit." He walked off into the night.

As if on cue, the line of luxury sedans and limos pulled up and whisked away the still silent and stony-faced glitterati. Nifoussi and Mizrahi were the last to step into their car. They both kissed me twice, and Abe snickered. "Don't look so tragic, Ally, darling, it pretty much happens every year. Call me." And they were gone. I looked back at Kamal, and he shrugged. "This year was like a shit show hat trick, but yeah, it pretty much does go south every time." He laughed.

"Why didn't you warn me?"

"What would be the fun in that?" He laughed, and I socked him playfully in the stomach. He threw his arm across my shoulders, and we headed back to our respective bunks. I didn't give a shit what anybody thought they were seeing, and that felt great for a change.

My bunk was eerily quiet when I pushed through the screen door. "Debbie," I whispered. "Are you here? Are you okay?"

It was quiet for a few seconds. Then a calm, flat voice replied, "Yes, I'm here."

"Are you okay? I mean, do you want to talk? I...well...it is none of my business, but if you want to talk...."

"What is there to say? And I think our little scene pretty much made it everyone's business." Her voice was quiet and steady. "I was his rebound. He groveled at her feet, and she dumped him, and it ripped him apart, and I was his rebound. And he wanted to drown himself in plain, boring me because he knew I would never leave him. He knew I thought I didn't deserve him. He used that to empower himself and make him feel whole again. And now she wants him back. They fucking deserve each other. And I deserve better."

"Wow. You got through two years of therapy in like thirty minutes. And of course, you are right. About all of it. And you do deserve better."

"Yeah. Still stings though. And I am really embarrassed I acted like such a smitten kitten all summer." She snorted a little laugh, "He is just so fucking hot. You know what I mean?"

"Yeah," I laughed, too. "He is."

"And the sex... you know what I mean?"

"Yeah, Debbie. I think I do."

"And Ally, I am sorry."

"For what?"

"For being such a judgy bitch about Kat and everything. It is none of my business."

"It's alright. I admit I was a little cavalier about Kat. I get she is just trying to get control over her situation, and I think people need control over their own lives. But I guess I underestimated how much innocent people can get hurt in these games." I smiled at her in the dark.

"Yeah. Sex, power, and ego." She sighed.

"And Debbie, I owe you another apology. I really am sorry," I teased.

"For what?"

"I am sorry that you mentioned how good the sex was with Andrik... because now I kind of want to fuck him! And I won't be able to think of anything else when I'm lying awake in bed tonight. *You know what I mean*?"

She laughed and threw her pillow at me. "Just for that, there is one more thing I think I need to tell you, Ally. I found a scorpion in your towel on the first night. Now you can just think about that when you are lying awake in bed. Sleep tight!"

I would not sleep at all ever again.

CHAPTER 13

EXODUS

Debbie and I woke up at the usual time and headed to the bathroom to wash up. She watched me eyeing my towel and winked. I thought better of it and grabbed a clean t-shirt to dry my face. We didn't speak until we were seated in the mess with the crew. Eyes darted back and forth nervously until I finally couldn't take it and blurted, "Are we likely to see Rob or Dicky this morning? I want to thank them and say my goodbyes."

It was Henry who smiled weakly and muttered, "Not likely."

I turned to Aggie, "And when will you be returning to Oxford, Aggie?"

"We, Dicky and I," she clarified, "have to stop in Istanbul at the end of this week and then I will... accompany him back to the UK. Simon ducked out last night. Before the... show. He wanted to get home. It is his little boy's first birthday today."

"Wow. How sweet. I wish I had a chance to say goodbye, but good for him."

"Yeah," Pano chimed in. "He was here last year when he was born. Four weeks early. His wife had an emergency C-section. They were both in the ICU for a few weeks. It nearly killed him."

"Oh God. I had no idea." Hearing that made me consider all that this lifestyle demanded.

These people flitted all over the world, which probably made making lasting connections difficult. And, if you were lucky enough to forge a "normal" life, you had to be prepared to occasionally walk away from it for weeks or months at a time.

Simon got home the day after his child was born but how terrifying it must have been for him and his wife to be separated even briefly not knowing if she and the child would survive, and Simon might be left to live with that grief and guilt.

I thought of my family. Sure, I missed my niece's first few months, but she would never know. I could still jump right in there and achieve cool aunt status.

And as for my parents, they just needed boundaries. I navigated this mess for seven weeks. I stood my ground. I survived rotting livestock, deadly footwear, spiteful gossip, and in the process managed to help a few people and make some new friends. I did not need their approval. There was shit happening in the world and in my head and in my life that they would never understand or accept. And I did not need them to.

Kamal appeared at the head of the table. "Until next year, people." He waved cheerfully and then went around the mess, hugging everyone and saying goodbye.

"Maybe next year, Lisa will join you," Tanya fished.

"Maybe." He wasn't biting. His eyes darted to mine for a moment, and he winked. And with that, he was gone. I rose and headed back toward the bunks by way of the kitchen.

"Don't get lost," Henry called after me. "We are leaving in fifteen minutes."

"Don't worry. I am just going to swing by the kitchen and see if Deniz has any baklava left over from last night. For the road. Since we are buds." I gave Philip a hard look.

Deniz was cleaning some eggplants for a meal I would be missing when I interrupted him with a cough.

"Hi. I just wanted to say goodbye. It was nice to meet you and thank you for all of the extra baklava." I smiled hopefully. "Is there any leftover? I would love to take some for the ride to Izmir. For me and a few others."

"Hi. Yes! Of course. Of course. I thought you would come." He stopped with the eggplants and dried his hands. "And Ali, thank you. For everything. Thank you for talking to Akara. You gave her light. Hope."

"Really, it was Kamal who talked to her...."

"Ali, it was you she saw. Another woman. Learning and making her own choices, living her true life. I don't know what will happen next. But you made her feel she was okay to want these things." He paused and took my hand. "Me too."

I took both of his hands and held them in mine. "Good luck. Be happy." It was all I could think to say. He nodded and handed me a box wrapped in paper. "Stay sweet, Miss Ali."

I took the box and went to grab my bags. I had chucked all of my gross clothing to cram my special rug into my duffel. My decision to leave my towel was based on other factors. There was a letter on my pillow. I unfolded it enough to see it was from Kamal. I shoved it in my carry-on to read on the plane. I grabbed my bag, my absurd hat, and the box of baklava I had no intention of sharing and headed for the driveway. I passed Debbie in the office on the phone trying to adjust her plans to meet up with some friends in Cyprus. She was going to travel, Andrik or not. Good for her. She blew me a kiss as I passed and mouthed, "I'll call you when I'm back in the City."

I rode to the airport in Izmir with Henry, Philip, and Tanya, who were staying in Istanbul for a few days. The plans were made a week ago, before the shit hit the fan, so it was a tense trip. Luckily, there was a rooster in a cage riding shotgun who seemed to have road rage and prevented us from having an uncomfortable silence.

On the plane, we were seated separately, so it was just a matter of saying our goodbyes quickly when we deplaned in Istanbul, and I would be alone.

"Sorry about last night, Ally. Sorry I was a dick all summer," started Philip as we parted. "I guess I was madder at you than I could admit to myself."

"It's okay. About last night and you being a dick all summer." We smiled at each other. "But now I realize it was partially my own fault. It wouldn't kill me to be a little more careful sometimes. And good luck! I am sure I will see you around The City." I looked past him at Tanya. "And have fun. Both of you." They headed toward baggage, and I hugged Henry.

"Thank you for everything, Henry. Good luck with the book, and don't let these people drive you nuts."

"Safe travels, Ally, and good luck to you, too. Don't worry about what is waiting for you back home. They should be worried about what is headed their way." We hugged again, and he ran to catch up with the others.

I turned and headed the other direction toward "connecting flights." I was totally spacing out and just following the traffic, getting in line, showing my paperwork, and having my documents stamped. I had my boarding pass and headed straight for security, which was within eyeshot of my gate. I was getting antsy. My flight would be called any second, and there was a bit of a line. My carry-on was scanned, and I heard a voice announce my flight was boarding.

Thank God. In the nick of time, but why was the security guy waving someone over and showing him my passport?

"Excuse me, sir. Is there a problem? My flight is boarding..."

"Miss, please come with us."

"Wait, why? I can't go anywhere. My flight is boarding. Please. I *cannot* miss my flight, sir." The two guys left me standing there. They took my passport and my boarding pass. Holy shit, holy shit! My heart was racing. Holy shit. It was like *Midnight Run*. I was going to prison. Did someone put drugs in my bag? Was my beautiful carpet a stolen antique? My carpet! It was jammed in my big backpack and was now under the plane. It would be all alone at JFK while I rotted in jail. Why the hell did they take my passport? Shit, they know I'm a Jew. My parents were right. Ugh, I'd rather go to prison than for that to be true! Should I tell them about the 500,000 Jews in Istanbul? Maybe they didn't know. The second guy was headed my way, looking very official.

"Where did you come from?"

"Originally?"

"No, miss, in Turkey."

"I was on the dig in Aphrodisias..."

"And then?"

"I flew from Izmir."

"When?"

"Today. Today I flew from Izmir." He looked at me suspiciously. Then his face softened. "They stamped your passport in Izmir. It is stamped saying you have already left Turkey."

"I am sorry, I don't understand. Please, sir, that was the final boarding call for my flight."

"Your passport says you already left Turkey earlier today."

"But I didn't. Clearly. I am trying to leave now." I don't know if it was the panic in my voice, the tears in my eyes, or the fact that he really didn't give a shit, but he shoved my documents in my face and nodded me away.

"Thank you! Thank you so much!" I called, sprinting toward the gate door that opened directly to the tarmac. Hot wind caught my hat, and I swear it lifted me halfway up the stairs to the plane. Breathless, I dropped into my seat just as we started moving. Within minutes we were in the air and Istanbul, then Turkey, and then the whole mess was behind me. It was safe to unpack the whole thing now from thirty thousand feet. Literally. I ordered a drink to knock back the sleeping pill Debbie gave me. It was from a pharmacy in Egypt. I was either going fall asleep or drop dead.

While I was still annoyed that it was only okay for me to let go of Philip when he decided to let go of me, I was glad he found Miss Right, or at least Miss Right Now, in Tanya. Gladder still for her to get over the whole Kamal situation. Especially since that was a dead end for a higher purpose. Well, nothing gets you over one guy like getting under another. Oh Ally. You are the worst.

I hoped for Ayeleen's sake that Kamal's subterfuge succeeded in getting her out of Turkey. Even with support from her entire family, it would take a good bit of chutzpah to make the move to the US and risk deportation and who knows what else to follow her dreams. Not to mention Akara. I had no sense of whether Kamal and I had actually helped her. Would a better understanding of what was possible in the world make her life better or worse if she really had no opportunity, access, or support from her family? Well, she had a brother who cared, and that was a start.

I really couldn't complain. My parents were certainly not encouraging or emotionally supportive, but they never said "no" or made it impossible for me to follow my dreams on my own steam. Further, I lived in a country where even as a single young woman, they had no legal right to do so. So that was that. No more apologizing and feeling guilty. No more looking outside for approval and validation. No more blaming other people's opinions for my lack of momentum. Time to grow up, girl.

And then the Egyptian sleeping pill kicked in, and I was out. For a long time.

When my eyes opened again, my face was pressed against the glass. Through the fog of my breath and drool, I could see The City looming large even from a distance.

Tears stung my eyes as I obeyed the command to fasten my seatbelt and straighten my seat. A few rough bumps and we then hit New York. Shazam!

I deplaned with the rest of the walking dead and headed to baggage, eager to retrieve the one item of value that actually belonged to me in my own right. After customs it would be time to complete my reentry and be collected by Phyllis and Howard.

And there they were. It was kisses and hugs and "You look great! Great color! You have everything, honey?" I did, so we were off.

We went straight to Quogue for the weekend. I was grateful for the space and time to run or take the car to sit by the dunes and stare across the Atlantic. Time to be alone. I told no one I was back. Even Mel. I would see them all next week at Stacie's wedding. I needed a few days to decompress.

Sitting on the beach alone, I reached into my bag for a smoke and found Kamal's letter. In the chaos that preceded my boarding in Istanbul, and the booze and pill-induced coma that followed, I had completely forgotten about it. I unfolded the paper and read it:

Dear Ally,

I hope this letter finds you well and safely on your way home. I wanted to tell you how happy I was to meet you this summer for so many reasons.

I know it was sometimes challenging for you feeling like an outsider on the dig. I saw the way Philip tried to make you suffer and punish you for wounding his ego, and I could punch him for it.

I felt in the same boat with Tanya. While I felt badly about the way things ended with us last year, I was more worried that she would overreact and try to blow up my situation.

Maybe that was selfish, but you never judged me for it.

You were a good friend to me. Good company and a great listener. I was really dreading coming home this summer to begin with. I had not yet told my parents I was married to an American and was planning to stay in the US indefinitely. Additionally, I was not sure how they would react when I told them I was taking Ayeleen back with me. I knew it would break their hearts, but really, I think it is best for us both.

You were so honest regarding your own struggles and doubts that you made it easy for me to talk about mine. Your vulnerability is one of your greatest strengths. Don't be ashamed of it.

And I admire the way you wanted to help Akara. To give her confidence and a voice.

I say this as your friend. You should take your own advice. The young woman I met this summer is strong enough to take on the haters, doubters, hell, the world! Fuck, she was strong enough to resist me, she must be Wonder Woman. Ha, ha.

So, until we meet again, continue to keep other people's secrets, have more faith in yourself, and get some more sensible shoes.

Your great admirer,

Kamal

CHAPTER 14

A FUNNY THING HAPPENED ON MY WAY TO GET WAXED....

Three days later, it was as if it never happened. I was hustling down Madison Avenue to Warren Tricomi after a long day of sending out resumes. Phyllis had booked me appointments for hair, nails, waxing, facial, a full decontamination, well in advance. I had to be completely groomed for my friends' weddings. Plus, I had a meeting next week with Abe Nifoussi. It was after six p.m., but the August humidity still had me huffing and puffing and schvitzing like mad.

As I hustled through a construction site, I was chatting with my sister on my new flip phone about my niece's poops. Apparently, while I was gone, phones became a "thing" in The City, and P and H took the liberty of getting me one for fear that failure to do so might result in my inability to get a job, or worse, a husband.

I could barely hear my sister's voice saying 'goodbye' over the jackhammer pounding the street as I click-clacked past a bodega featuring the latest edition of *Life Magazine*. Through the dust cloud, I spotted a picture of the theater at Aphrodisias on the cover. I was so distracted I didn't see the subway grate that caught the kitten heel on my Prada sandal, and before I knew it, I was face down on the pavement. My Jackie O's flew off my face, and the big, stupid hat was knocked right off my head. Foiled by foot fashion again. I was out for fifteen seconds at least and forgot where I was. I heard a deep baritone somewhere. Was it the call to prayer? No. A voice said, "Are you okay? Are you hurt?" I turned my head and squinted at the suit extending an outstretched hand in my direction. I scrambled up on my own steam and noticed he was cute. He kind of looked like a better-looking Jerry Seinfeld. No mullet. He must have come from some conference or something because he had a "Hi, my name is Paul" sticker still clinging limply to his lapel.

"Are you okay?" he repeated. "That was quite an impressive faceplant." He joked, handing me the hat and the glasses.

"Thank you, Paul." I read from his sticker as I brushed the dirt from my sweaty face, hands, and body and popped back on the shades. I looked from the bustling street around me to the clear sky above and then into his pretty blue eyes. "I just got distracted and didn't see where I was going. Really. I am fine. I am used to a little dirt," I said with a giggle.

"You sure? You don't look like the type of girl that likes to be dirty." He heard it as soon as he said it. "I mean likes to get dirty. I mean you look like a nice clean girl. I'm sorry." He was so flustered. It was really cute. "I didn't get your name?"

"Ally. My name is Ally." I extended a dusty hand for him to shake.

"Ally," he repeated. "Are you sure you are okay, Ally?" He said my name like a wish as he shook my hand and used his other to straighten my glasses.

"Yes. Thank you." My eyes looked away from his to the

waning sun starting to dip behind the taller buildings on the west side of the street, and I remembered my appointments.

I looked back at him. "I am surprised to hear myself say it, Paul, but I'm one hundred percent confident I'm going to be just fine." I tipped my head and winked over my shades at him as I walked away. I could feel him watching me disappear into the crowd. I had this excited feeling that while one chapter of my life was closing, another more exciting one was about to begin. Sure, I was a little bruised, but I was battle-tested and more determined than ever.

ACKNOWLEDGEMENTS

I want to thank Orange Hat publishing for believing in me and my story. Most of all I want to thank my family who listened to me talk about first writing, then publishing and finally promoting this book for the better part of forever. Paul, Jack and Izzie, I love you.

www.ingramcontent.com/pod-product-compliance
Lightning Source LLC
LaVergne TN
LVHW030920080826
845145LV00013B/2980

* 9 7 8 1 6 4 5 3 8 6 4 2 1 *